D0987904

Snakes'
Elbows

ORCHARD BOOKS
96 Leonard Street, London EC2A 4XD
Orchard Books Australia
32/45-51 Huntley Street, Alexandria, NSW 2015
First published in Great Britain in 2005
First paperback edition 2006
Text © Deirdre Madden 2005
Illustrations © Tony Ross 2005
The right of Deirdre Madden to be identified as the author and
Tony Ross to be identified as the illustrator have
been asserted by them in accordance with the
Copyright, Designs and Patents Act, 1988.
A CIP catalogue record for this book is available
from the British Library.
ISBN 1 84362 639 X (hardback)
ISBN 1 84362 640 3 (paperback)
1 3 5 7 9 10 8 6 4 2 (hardback)
1 3 5 7 9 10 8 6 4 2 (paperback)
Printed in Great Britain

Snakes' Elbows

DEIRDRE MADDEN

ORCHARD BOOKS

898, 187|

For Brigitte Fabre, with love

THE LITTLE TOWN

The story I am about to tell you took place in Woodford, a most unremarkable little town – or so it seemed. It had the usual shops and houses and offices, factories and parks and churches. A slow river flowed through the centre, spanned by a series of stout stone bridges and at the edge of the town there was a dark forest. Beyond that again there was a mountain, but it was not particularly high or famous or important or beautiful. Like the town, it was quite unremarkable: it was just a mountain.

Had you asked any of the citizens of Woodford what was special about it, I doubt if any of them would have been able to answer you straight off. There would have been quite a bit of head-scratching and humming and hawing. 'Now let me see,' they'd likely have said. And then they would probably have mentioned the church: not

Saint John's, the modern one, but the other one, which was very old. How old? Your average Woodford man or woman probably didn't know. 'Oh, ancient,' they would say if you pressed them. 'Hundreds and hundreds of years old.' It had stained-glass windows that didn't show angels or saints but wild flowers: primroses in one pointed window, violets in another, harebells in another and so on. On a frosty afternoon in February when the light is at its best for looking at such things, they glowed like jewels in the darkness of the church and reminded the people, who were cold and tired at the end of winter, that the Spring would come again soon, bringing real flowers to the fields and to the forest: primroses and violets and harebells.

Of what else would the citizens have spoken? They might have mentioned that in the middle of the main square was an imposing statue of Albert Hawkes, the little town's most famous son. 'Born in Woodford. Died in Glory' it said on the plinth; and generations of children thought that Glory must be the name of the far-off city in which Albert Hawkes had ended his days. But there was, unfortunately, a slight problem: no one had the foggiest idea who Albert Hawkes was and what he had done to merit such a grand statue. Was he a military man who had won a famous victory? Probably not, because then the statue would have shown him in uniform, waving a sword in the air. Perhaps he was a learned man, a professor or even a poet, but then he would have been holding a bronze book in his bronze hands. An inventor? Then why wasn't he holding the thing he had invented? Albert Hawkes' statue gave no clues to who he had been. It showed him as a man of medium height with a frock coat and a splendid moustache, leaning on a broken pillar with his chin propped in his right hand. He was gazing off into the middle distance with a slightly puzzled expression. You could have been forgiven for thinking that even he had forgotten who he was, and was trying his best to remember.

The people of Woodford didn't even think of him as Albert Hawkes, and had long since stopped wondering what he had done to be famous. They simply spoke of The Statue and used it as a place to meet before heading along to do something more interesting, such as going to the cinema or to an ice-cream parlour. The

Statue was a bus terminus. I hate to have to tell you this, but the odd passing dog used to lift its leg against the plinth and no one thought this an outrage or indeed cared at all. There are many people who spend their lives desperately trying to be famous: they should think about the fate of Albert Hawkes.

The town did have an art gallery but I doubt if anyone would have mentioned it, because unfortunately the paintings in it were not good. Not good at all. In fact they were completely hopeless. They looked as if when they had been painted, the artists had had a bad headache or tummy ache; or perhaps simply their minds had been elsewhere and they had been wondering what was for tea that night or if the postman would bring something interesting.

Anything else? Yes, Woodford Creams! They would certainly have told you about Woodford Creams, which are chocolates with a rose-scented cream-filled centre that are every bit as delicious as they sound, and horribly expensive. They were sold from a shop the size of a large suitcase, by the shy, dreamy woman whose mother had invented the chocolates and who had given her daughter the secret recipe. The people of Woodford bought them as gifts or as treats for themselves. At Christmas time there was always a queue out the door of the shop, down the street, around the corner, sometimes even as far as The Statue. (And if you knew Woodford you would realise that that is a very long way indeed.)

And so already you can see that even though it was a most unremarkable little town, there were things in it that were interesting and delicious and delightful. This is true of every town no matter how dull it may at first appear to be. Of course if you have absolutely no curiosity or imagination whatsoever, even the most exciting city in the world will seem boring to you. But if you do open your eyes wide and look at what is there under your very nose, you will find wonders and marvels even in a completely ordinary place like Woodford.

But wait! How could I possibly have forgotten Jasper? Jasper Jellit was an extravagant and flamboyant millionaire who lived in a flashy great mansion at the edge of town. He threw wild parties and the people of Woodford were completely and utterly fascinated by him. 'Not every town has someone like Jasper living in it,' they'd have said, although the wiser folk would perhaps have pointed out that this was something of a mixed blessing. On the day this story begins, however, it wasn't Jasper they were thinking about. At the church and in the chocolate shop, in the art gallery and among the groups of people standing around The Statue, waiting to meet their friends or to catch a bus, there was tremendous excitement. 'Have you heard?' they said to each other. 'Have you heard the news?' There was one topic of conversation that day and only one, which was this:

Barney Barrington was coming back to live in Woodford.

THE WOODFORD TRUMPET

The people knew this because they had read about it in the *Woodford Trumpet*, a small, loud newspaper with lots of photographs and great big headlines. It also had a rather odd habit of putting some words in BLOCK CAPITALS, so that it looked like THIS. Perhaps they thought their READERS were too BUSY to read the paper SLOWLY, and in glancing over the main WORDS they would get the general IDEA. Perhaps they thought their EYESIGHT was BAD. Perhaps they even thought that their READERS were a bit DIM.

Whatever the reason, the headline that morning read: 'MUSICAL MILLIONAIRE COMES HOME TO WOODFORD!' And then in smaller print it said, 'See pages 2, 3, 4, 5, 6 & 7.' This didn't leave much room for any other news, which was a pity, because lots of important if rather unexciting things were happening at that time.

'After YEARS away,' the paper said on its front page, 'Pianist BARNEY BARRINGTON is coming back to LIVE in WOODFORD. (I'll drop the capitals from here on out if you don't mind. You're probably not BUSY and I'm certain you're not DIM and even if your EYESIGHT is BAD (mine is terrible) I doubt if CAPITALS will HELP.)

'Millionaire Barney, who is even richer than Jasper Jellit, has bought The Oaks and is expected to move in any day now. Child genius Barney left Woodford when he was only five. The piano-playing sprog went on to stun the world with his skill on the ivories. Now, more than sixty years later, he is coming back to live here again. And who can blame him, eh? Good on yer, Barney! Welcome Home!'

Above this there were two large photographs. One showed a frail, rather anxious little child with soft fair hair standing beside an immense black grand piano. 'Nimble-fingered nipper: Barney at six,' the caption read. The other photo showed a frail, rather anxious looking elderly man with soft grey hair, standing beside an immense black grand piano. 'Still packing 'em in,' it said below.

'Barney wowing New York last week.'

The rest of the paper was full of pictures and stories about Barney. The *Trumpet* said that he had never had a home since leaving Woodford, but had spent all his life travelling the world, staying in hotels and giving concerts. They told about the zillions and squillions of records he had sold and of how sometimes there had been punch-ups at the box office when there weren't enough concert tickets to go round. They said how quiet and shy he had been as a child and how he had never changed. There were photos of him in London and Tokyo and Sydney and Paris.

'Snakes' elbows! Richer than me?' Jasper Jellit was sitting up in bed in his ruby silk pyjamas reading the paper and eating a soft-boiled egg with toast soldiers, his Tuesday morning breakfast. He was a picky eater and had a different breakfast brought to him, cooked just so, every day in the week. 'RICHER THAN ME??!!!'

He shouted so loud that he woke up his two Alsatian dogs, Cannibal and Bruiser, who were snoozing in their basket at the foot of the bed.

'Oh what is it this time?' they thought crossly. 'There's no need to make such a racket.'

Jasper leafed wildly through the paper looking for news about himself. There was always something. The morning after one of his incredible parties there would be pages and pages of photographs in all of which Jasper appeared, and reports in which the guests said how it was the best party they had ever been to in their entire lives and how Jasper was the most wonderful person they had ever met. Often he would pull some stunt just to get attention. One day, for example, he went out and bought up every single Woodford Cream in the shop. It was the most anyone had ever bought at one go and it was all over the *Woodford Trumpet* the next day. There were far too many for him to eat himself and he fed some of them to Cannibal and Bruiser, even though he knew you should never give chocolate to dogs. He was curious to know how sick it would make them: it made them very sick indeed.

But there was nothing about him in the paper today, nothing at all. Everything was about Barney Barrington.

'What's wrong with him now?' Cannibal wondered.

'He's gone the same colour as his pyjamas,' thought Bruiser.

Jasper threw his paper aside and jumped out of bed, sending the toast soldiers flying. He picked up the phone and rang his butler.

'Come here,' he said. Jasper rarely bothered with details such as saying 'Please' or 'Thank you' or even 'Hello'.

'Come here IMMEDIATELY. You're going to help me to plan the biggest and best, the most incredible and amazing party that Woodford has ever seen.'

Cannibal and Bruiser looked at each other in dismay. 'Oh no!' they thought. 'Oh no. Here we go again.'

Meanwhile, over at The Oaks, Barney Barrington was quietly moving into his new home.

BARNEY'S FIRST DAY BACK

Woodford was not as Barney remembered it. He hadn't been back since he was five. It wasn't so much that things had changed, it was just that they looked different now that he was older. Take the river that flowed through the middle of the town. When Barney was small it had seemed to him like a raging torrent. If you fell into it, he thought, you would be carried away in moments and never seen again. He had been too little to see over the bridges and his mother used to lift him up and set him on the parapet so that he could look down into the waters as they swept past below. It had been frightening in a way because of the strong current and the depth; but nice too, because his mother had always held on to him tightly and he knew he wouldn't fall in. He clung to her arms and watched the river race past.

Now that he was grown up, he could easily

898, 187

look over the side of the bridges without help as he walked through the town for the first time in over sixty years. He was amazed to see how narrow the river seemed, how small and slow and shallow. This was partly because when he was a child it was the only river he had ever known, but during his life he had found out just how big a river can be. Barney had seen the Seine in Paris and the Thames in London. He had seen immense rivers: the Mississippi when he was in the United States, the Nile in Egypt and the Ganges in India. When he was in Brazil he had even seen the Amazon, which was so wide that when you stood on one bank you couldn't see the other side.

But the river in Woodford also looked small now simply because Barney himself was bigger. The statue of Albert Hawkes was also not as big as he had thought it. Neither the mountain at the edge of the town nor the spire of the church, the one with the pretty windows, was as high as he remembered. He felt a little as if he were looking at everything in the town through the wrong end of a telescope. And although he understood why this should be, it made him feel slightly sad.

His first day in Woodford did not go well. He

WESTMEATH COUNTY LIBRARY

went into the art gallery because apart from playing the piano, Barney loved looking at paintings more than anything else in the world. But the Woodford pictures were so disappointing. There was one where the sheep were bigger than the shepherd, and a portrait of a lady who was rather beautiful except that she had her eyes crossed. Barney guessed correctly that this wasn't deliberate, but that the painter, although extremely good at hands and hair, was not very skilful when it came to eyes. 'Oh well,' Barney thought, 'at least I have paintings of my own to look at.'

From the gallery, he went to the supermarket to buy some food. The kitchen of the house into which he had moved was completely empty and so he needed everything. He would have to carry home all the boring things like salt and tea before he could even begin to think of treats like jam tarts and chocolate cake. Because he had spent all his life in hotels he had never had to shop for groceries before and he found it bewildering, all the aisles stuffed with packets and tins of every kind of food you could imagine. Just as he was putting a sliced loaf in his basket he heard someone saying, 'It's him! Barney Barrington! The pianist!' Embarrassed, Barney slipped into the next aisle and went on with his shopping.

'Look, Ma!' a little boy said. 'That man with the can of soup and the milk! It's the man who was in the paper this morning, the millionaire who's come back to live here.'

Everyone who was standing around with yoghurts and eggs and pieces of cheese in their hands stopped what they were doing and turned to stare at Barney, as though he were one of the paintings in Woodford's art gallery.

'He's right, you know,' said an old man. 'It is him.'

Barney felt his face go hot and red. Even though he didn't have everything he needed or wanted he hurried to the check-out.

'Oh look,' said the young woman behind the till, 'it's you! It's him,' she said to the man behind Barney as she rang up the groceries.

'Who?' said the man.

'Him,' said the young woman. 'You know, whassisname. Thingie. The fellow in the paper. Plays the piano. Pots of money. It is you, isn't it?' she said, turning to Barney again.

'Yes, it's me,' Barney confessed helplessly.

'Told you so,' the young woman said triumphantly to the man in the queue.

Barney paid for his shopping and fled.

By the time he got home he was ready for lunch. He made beans on toast, but he could see that it wasn't going to be very nice because he had forgotten to get any butter for the bread. He decided to eat up in his room and was crossing the hall with his meal on a tray when suddenly the doorbell rang. Who could it possibly be? He didn't know anyone in Woodford. He set his lunch on the hall table and cautiously opened the front door.

Plooff! Immediately a flashgun went off, blinding Barney for a moment with its white light.

'Who are you?' he exclaimed to the two men who were standing on his front step.

'*Woodford Trumpet,*' said one, as *Plooff!* The second man took another photograph.

'I don't want my picture taken,' Barney said, and as he moved to close the door the man who had spoken shoved his foot in to block it open. The foot was wearing a splendid shiny black shoe of the finest leather. This was odd because otherwise the man was extremely scruffy.

'*Woodford Trumpet,*' he said again. 'Come on, open up.'

'What do you want?' asked Barney.

'Tell us all about your fabulous life. Show us round your lovely home, you know. All that.'

'I'd rather not, if you don't mind,' Barney said.

'Well, I *do* mind, as a matter of fact,' the man replied, becoming shirty. 'I haven't got all day to waste, I'm due over at Jasper Jellit's place in an hour's time to see the preparations for his party. Come on, hurry up and let us in.'

By now Barney felt quite frightened. 'I really don't want to,' he said again.

The man was still pushing at the door with his foot and peering through the gap to see whatever he could of the house. Suddenly he spotted the tray sitting on the hall table. 'That your lunch?' he demanded incredulously. 'Beans on toast? That's all you're having? No smoked salmon? No champagne?'

'I don't like smoked salmon,' Barney said. 'I like beans on toast.'

Plooff! The man with the camera had stuck a

long lens through the gap in the door and taken another photo. The blinding light startled his companion who made the mistake of moving his foot.

Immediately, Barney slammed the door and turned the key, locking them out. His heart was pounding with fear.

The man from the *Woodford Trumpet* began to hammer and bang. 'Oi! You! That's not fair! Let me in! Open this door or you'll be sorry.' The knocking went on and on, ending with a last blow so violent that Barney guessed correctly that the man had kicked the door with his splendid shiny black shoe of the finest leather. 'Don't think you've heard the last of this because you haven't,' he shouted through the letterbox. 'You'll be sorry!'

By the time all of this was over Barney's baked beans were stone cold. He returned to the kitchen and scraped them back into the pot to warm them up again but it wasn't a success because of all the crumbs from the toast that were mixed in with the tomato sauce. Eventually Barney gave up.

He went to his room where his piano was. No matter how bad he was feeling, even if the weather was cold and wet, even if he was lonely and people were being horrible to him, playing the piano always made him feel better. He loved listening to beautiful music, and to make that music, to be at the centre of that wonderful sound, to be a part of it, was the sweetest thing. And so opening his piano Barney started to play. Although he did not know it, something was to happen the following day that would completely change his life.

WILF

When he was in town doing his shopping, Barney had asked to have the newspaper delivered to his house every day, and so when he went downstairs the following morning there was a copy of the *Woodford Trumpet* lying on the doormat.

'WE SPILL THE BEANS ON BARMY BARNEY!' screamed the headline. Below this there was a photograph of the plate of beans on toast Barney had been going to have for his lunch the previous day.

'THE *WOODFORD TRUMPET* can reveal today that MAD millionaire Barney Barrington is a SKINFLINT!

'"I LOVE smoked salmon," the parsimonious pianist told our special reporter yesterday in an EXCLUSIVE interview. "But it COSTS too much. So I eat baked beans. I don't LIKE them, but at least they're CHEAP!"'

On the front page there was also a picture of a devilishly handsome man standing outside a white marquee with two big black Alsatians. 'IT'S GOING TO BE A BIG ONE!' read the caption, and then in slightly smaller print: 'JASPER JELLIT, seen here with his DOGS Cannibal and Bruiser, tells the *Trumpet* EVERYTHING about his plans for this weekend's INCREDIBLE party! Please see pages 2, 3, 4, 5 & 6.'

Feeling rather glum, Barney went into the kitchen and made his breakfast, which was not a success. He was carrying it through the hall on a tray when suddenly the doorbell rang.

'Oh no! Not again!'

His heart began to thump and he stood still, hoping whoever was there would simply go away. But the doorbell rang again and suddenly the flap of the letterbox shot up, revealing a pair of small bright eyes. 'So you are at home after all,' said a voice.

'Please go away,' Barney pleaded.

'Couldn't we talk for a moment? I just wanted to ask you something.'

'Are you a journalist?'

'Me? No! Course not!'

'Who are you then?'

The small bright eyes blinked. 'It doesn't matter,' the voice said sadly. 'I'd best be on my way. People are always telling me to push off. Sorry to disturb you. It was just a thought.' The flap of the letterbox snapped shut and the small bright eyes disappeared.

'Stop! Wait!' Barney put his tray down and threw open the front door.

Standing on the doorstep was a roly-poly little man with wild hair and small bright eyes. He looked humorous and jolly and made no move to shove his foot in the door. 'Hello!' he said. 'My name's Wilf. I was just wondering if there was any chance of a job going.'

'What kind of a job?' said Barney.

'Anything really,' Wilf said. 'I suppose I'm a bit late in the day, you've probably got loads of people working for you by now. I could mow your lawn or if you needed any painting or decorating I could do it. I can turn my hand to anything, me.'

Even though he was no good at anything except playing the piano, it had never crossed Barney's mind to employ anyone. But now that Wilf had suggested it, it seemed like a wonderful idea.

Suddenly Wilf spotted the tray of food. 'That your breakfast?' Barney nodded. 'Doesn't look too tasty, does it? You've burnt your toast.'

'I know,' Barney said sadly.

'And you've cut it into squares. Toast's nicer when you cut it into triangles. If I came to work for you, I'd bring you your breakfast every morning.'

'What would you give me?'

'Whatever you wanted.'

'That's part of the problem,' Barney sighed. 'I never know what I want. I'm so indecisive.'

'Let me see then,' Wilf said. 'Some days I'd bring you crumpets that I'd toasted until they were piping hot and I'd cover them with butter that would melt and drip through the holes. Then I'd sprinkle them with cinnamon and sugar. Other times I'd bring you cornflakes and a white china pot full of hot chocolate. Some mornings I'd even make you pancakes.'

'What about lunch? Would you give me nice lunches too? And dinners?'

'Course I would.'

'And would you ever give me spinach or sprouts?'

'Yuk! No! Never!' said Wilf.

'When can you start?' asked Barney.

Wilf started to work for Barney that very day. He went down to the supermarket and bought all the things that had been forgotten the day before. Although he was a small man he was extremely strong and he carried home a massive bag of shopping. At noon he made mashed potatoes with roast chicken and peas, and afterwards there was lemon pudding and cream. Barney was desperately hungry. He hadn't had a proper meal since arriving in Woodford, what with the cold baked beans and the burnt toast, and he thought Wilf's lunch was the most delicious thing he had eaten in years.

In the early afternoon, just after Wilf had finished doing the dishes, a huge lorry pulled up outside the house.

'What's this all about?'

'It's my collection of paintings,' Barney said anxiously as the men started to unload dozens of big wooden packing cases. To his great relief, Wilf immediately took charge, telling them where to put the boxes as they were brought into the house. After the men had gone, Barney and Wilf spent the rest of the day opening the cases and hanging the paintings on the walls. Wilf drilled holes and hammered in nails. With all the hard work, his hair became even wilder than it had been when he arrived at the house that morning, and stood straight up in mad tufts. He prised open each of the packing cases in turn and carefully lifted out the pictures.

Barney loved his paintings so much. Seeing them again was like meeting old friends after many years. Because he had spent all his life living in hotels he had only ever been able to have one painting with him at any given time and the others had been kept in store until today. Taking them out of their boxes was like opening presents; it was like Christmas and his birthday all rolled into one. Some of the pictures were huge and filled a whole wall. Some were tiny and looked as if they had been painted using a brush with only one hair. There was the painting of a ship sailing off into the sunset. There was the castle on a cliff beside the sea. There was the beautiful woman with a yellow butterfly balanced on the tip of her finger – oh, there were so many of them, more than I could ever tell you, and each one was more wonderful than the one before.

When all the paintings with their gold frames were on the walls, Wilf made them both an evening meal of cheese sandwiches and chocolate biscuits with orange juice. Barney had really enjoyed the day, unlike yesterday, when he had felt so lonely and miserable. 'Will you come and work for me, Wilf?' he asked as they were drinking their juice. 'Will you help me with everything? You can live here if you want because there are lots of empty rooms.' He also told Wilf that he would pay him and when he said how much, Wilf's eyes opened wide.

'As much as that? Are you sure?'

'Certain,' Barney said.

'Done deal! Yippee!'

Wilf was so pleased that even his hair looked happy.

JASPER'S PARTY

Meanwhile over at Jasper's house, plans were proceeding for the big bash on Saturday night. It wasn't just Cannibal and Bruiser who hated it when he threw a party; everybody who worked for him hated it too. Jasper was not a sweet-tempered man at the best of times but now he was unbearable. 'Look at the state of that lawn!' he screamed at the gardener. 'Call that a cake, do you?' he thundered at the pastry cook. 'You think that's good wine?' he bellowed at the cellar man.

The odd thing about this was that everything was perfect. The lawn looked like a billiard table. The airy cake was light and delicious. The bottle of wine was fragrant and sweet. But none of this stopped Jasper from working himself up into a complete tantrum, throwing himself down and screeching and howling.

'Oh grow up, for goodness sake,' Cannibal and

Bruiser thought as they watched him hammering on the ground with his feet and his fists.

All of Jasper's parties had a theme. At the most recent one, all the guests had been told to dress up as animals. Jasper himself had gone as a parrot. He had worn an extraordinary costume made of thousands and thousands of brightly coloured feathers, all sewn together by hand (although not, of course, by Jasper). At the back was a long green feathery tail that trailed the ground when he walked. As you might imagine, he looked like a complete twit. Because all the people at the party were dressed as animals – mice and rabbits and monkeys and cats – Jasper thought it would be hilarious if the animals at the party were dressed as people. He therefore, at great expense, had some clothes made for the two dogs. Cannibal was forced to wear a three-piece pinstriped suit with a shirt and tie. Jasper even had a jeweller make Cannibal a little pocket watch on a chain. Poor Bruiser had to put on a small silk frock printed with roses and with a wide pink sash. How the guests laughed when they saw the two dogs! Even the ones who didn't think it was funny pretended that they did because they were afraid of Jasper.

'Don't they look ridiculous! Isn't it a hoot!'

The circus party had been even worse although to begin with it hadn't seemed so, for Cannibal and Bruiser had only had to wear small frilly collars like circus dogs and pointy hats. Jasper was dressed as a ringmaster, complete with a top hat, a red satin jacket and a long leather whip. The whole house and garden had been turned into a circus. There were acrobats in the library and a lion tamer in the conservatory. There were fire-eaters on the lawn, a dancing bear in the front hall and everywhere there were clowns.

Although there was lots of good food, Cannibal and Bruiser weren't given any because all the guests were under strict instructions not to feed the dogs. The guests knew that if they broke this rule they risked being thrown out immediately and never invited to any of Jasper's parties ever again. Jasper always kept the dogs hungry to make them bad-tempered. He liked the idea of being seen out and about with two mad snarling Alsatians because it would make him look frightening and Jasper loved to think that people were scared of him. Cannibal and Bruiser were such good-natured dogs however that they didn't become black-hearted no matter how mean Jasper was to them. They spent most of their lives trailing around behind him in a deep sulk.

On the night of the circus party they wandered around the house and grounds, sticking together and looking out for each other.

'Careful, Cannibal!' Bruiser said, as a trick cyclist whizzed past, missing his companion by a whisker.

'Mind out, Bruiser,' Cannibal exclaimed, as a spinning plate fell off a pole and smashed to the ground, almost hitting his friend on the head.

And then suddenly behind them, *Raakk!* Someone had cracked a whip. The two dogs looked at each other in fright. *Raakk!* 'What will we do?' Cannibal asked.

'Run,' Bruiser said. 'RUN!'

Raakk! The dogs ran and ran as fast as they possibly could to try to get away, but ahead of them now someone was holding up a hoop. Now this would have been no problem whatsoever except for one minor detail: the hoop was on fire. It was a perfect circle of flickering orange flames against the night sky and they could feel the heat of it already on their snouts because, still running at full pelt, Cannibal and Bruiser were heading straight for it!

'What will we do?' Bruiser asked.

'Jump,' Cannibal said. 'JUMP!'

Side by side and more terrified than they had ever been in all their lives, the two dogs leapt through the blazing hoop. They made it, but it was a tight fit. Cannibal's collar was slightly burnt on the right-hand side and the hair on Bruiser's left flank was scorched. Trembling and panting, they collapsed on the grass. All around them was a huge crowd of people laughing and clapping their hands, congratulating Jasper and telling him how clever he was. For as you may have guessed by now, it was he who had both cracked the whip and held up the hoop. Yes, as far as Cannibal and Bruiser were concerned, the circus party had definitely been the worst so far.

On Wednesday morning the postman made a special delivery to over two hundred people in Woodford. He brought them a long flat white box tied with a green ribbon and inside each box was a bar of milk chocolate. PARTY! was written on it in white chocolate, and then below that:

'Jasper Jellit requests the pleasure of your

company this Saturday night at his amazing, unbelievable, no-expense-spared, once-in-a-lifetime, never-before-seen-in-Woodford-nor indeed-anywhere-else-for-that-matter CHOCOLATE PARTY!!!' Below that again was added, 'Eight o'clock sharp. Posh frocks and best suits essential.'

All the guests were terribly excited. 'There'll be a chocolate pudding as big as a bus,' they said to each other on their way on the party on Saturday night, dressed up to the nines. 'There'll be great pyramids of Woodford Creams all over the place. Buckets of chocolate ice cream. Chocolate biscuits and chocolate toffee and chocolate fudge and chocolate gateau and chocolate creams and simply hundreds and hundreds of bars of chocolate!' And do you know what? All the guests were completely...

Wrong!

At eight on the dot, two trumpet players came out on to the top step of the white marble staircase that led to the front door of Jasper's flashy great mansion. They blew a fanfare and all the guests who were milling around on the lawn below fell silent. Then the front door of the house flew open and there was Jasper, looking rather dashing in his dinner jacket, with Cannibal and Bruiser on either side of him.

'Welcome, friends, welcome!' he cried, after the applause had died down. 'I am delighted that you have all been able to come to my party and I promise you a night to remember. When you are weary old folk with grey hair and boring lives you will still be able to impress people by telling them that you were here tonight, because this is a party that is going to go down in history. And so without further ado, let the Great Chocolate Party begin!'

Immediately the gardens were all lit up and the fountains came on. And suddenly the air was full of the smell of hot chocolate, because that was what was flowing through Jasper's three fountains this evening instead of water. There was one fountain of white chocolate, one of milk and one of plain. The guests also noticed that there were lots of new statues scattered about the lawn and they too were made of chocolate. There was a whole orchard that had been put in place for that night only and from the branches of the trees hung pears and apples made of chocolate. In the flowerbeds were chocolate roses and snapdragons and lilies. 'Help yourselves!' Jasper cried. 'Have fun!'

To begin with, it was all very well-behaved. Beside each fountain stood servants with china cups so that the guests could fill them with the hot chocolate if they wished to drink. There were also baskets of strawberries and marshmallows, biscuits and tiny cakes, together with long forks so that the guests could dip them in the basins of the fountains and coat them in chocolate before eating them. 'How clever of Jasper!' they said as they politely waited their turn. 'Always so original. Always so imaginative,' and they snapped off a chocolate rose or two and nibbled on them delicately.

Cannibal and Bruiser slunk around the garden hoping they wouldn't be noticed. They hadn't forgotten the day Jasper had fed them the Woodford Creams. Someone licked the toes of a statue standing nearby. 'It really is made of chocolate,' she said, 'the best chocolate I've ever eaten in my whole life.'

As time went on, the guests' manners began to slip. They dipped their fingers in the liquid chocolate of the fountains and licked them, then their whole hands. They dived head first into the rose bushes and gorged themselves on the chocolate flowers. Instead of reaching up into the branches to pull a single pear or apple made of chocolate, they climbed up into the trees and shook them until dozens of fruits tumbled into the grass below. The two dogs watched in dismay to see how greedy people can be, as the guests snapped off whole arms and legs from the statues and crept away to guzzle them alone. By this time some of them were even being sick behind the bushes because they had eaten so much.

'Tee hee! This will be a lark!'

Before Cannibal and Bruiser knew what was happening, some guests had sneaked up behind them, grabbed them and *Splash!* – thrown them in the fountains.

'Help! Help!' Cannibal cried to his friend as he struggled not to sink in the basin of hot white chocolate. But there was nothing Bruiser could do, because she was thrashing around in the fountain that was full of hot dark chocolate. 'Don't open your mouth! Don't swallow any and whatever you do, don't lick yourself!'

With enormous difficulty the two dogs

eventually managed to heave themselves out of the fountains, but not before they were both completely covered in chocolate. How Jasper and the guests howled with laughter to see them, one white and one plain! And then they simply walked away and forgot about them. Cannibal and Bruiser felt the chocolate harden around them.

'It's as if I'm turning to stone,' Cannibal said.

'There's nothing we can do but wait for someone to come and help us,' Bruiser replied.

The night went on and the mad party finally came to an end. The last chocolate-crazed guest departed and Jasper went to his bed, tired but happy. By that time the chocolate coating on the two dogs had set solid and they couldn't budge an inch. It was the following morning before some servants, cleaning up the terrible mess in the garden, came upon Cannibal and Bruiser and took pity on them. They carried the dogs into the kitchen and set them each in turn above a pot of warm water until the chocolate began to melt and drip off them, until each of them was standing in a pool of liquid chocolate and was free again.

'That does it,' Cannibal said as soon as he had recovered. 'I've had enough of Jasper Jellit.'

'Don't worry, we'll get our own back on him for this, in our own time, in our own way,' Bruiser added. 'Just see if we don't!'

DANDELION

The arrangement that Wilf should work for Barney went brilliantly right from the start. At the end of the first week, the men from the *Woodford Trumpet* came back and this time it wasn't Barney who received them.

Plooff! Wilf managed to cover his face just in time. The journalist tried to put his nicely shod foot in the door again, but Wilf was faster and stronger than Barney and slammed it closed.

'Oi! That hurt!' the man yelped out on the step, and then he began to hammer and bang angrily on the door. 'Who do you think you are anyway? Open up. It's Mr Barrington I want to talk to.'

'He doesn't want to talk to you. Go away.' Wilf knelt down, lifted up the flap and peeped through the letterbox.

Plooff!

'I'm looking after Mr Barrington now. Go away,' he said again. 'You heard me. Hoppit.'

Standing at the top of the stairs, Barney was listening to all of this. His heart was thumping, but he knew he was safe. He didn't know what he was most grateful for: Wilf's wonderful cooking or the way he protected him from people like the men from the *Woodford Trumpet*.

The following morning Wilf brought Barney his breakfast as usual. On the trolley he wheeled into the room was a pot of tea, toast (cut into triangles and not burnt), pats of butter and lemon marmalade. There were bread rolls and two kinds of jam, raspberry and apricot. There was freshly squeezed orange juice and under a round silver dome there were crisp rashers, plump sausages and two perfectly fried eggs.

'This looks delicious!' Barney said happily as he poured his tea.

'I hope you enjoy it.' Wilf looked extremely glum this morning. His eyes had lost their sparkle and his hair was completely flat. 'I made a special effort because it's the last meal I'll be making for you. I'm leaving.'

'What?!!' Barney was so shocked he almost

dropped the teapot. 'Why, Wilf? What's the matter? Aren't you happy here with me?'

'I love it. Never been happier in my life, but I have to go. You won't want me to stay after you've read this.' Wilf held out a copy of the *Woodford Trumpet* to Barney, who took it and unfolded it.

'MAD MILLIONAIRE HIRES HOMELESS HOOLIGAN!'

Below this were two odd photographs. One showed a face covered by an outspread hand and framed by wild, spiky hair. The other showed two small bright eyes peeping through a letterbox. 'The *Woodford Trumpet* has DISCOVERED and can reveal exclusively to our readers that BATTY Barney Barrington's new butler is a ROOFLESS RUFFIAN and a JAILBIRD! Before moving in with the mean millionaire, Wilf Wilson had NO JOB and NO HOUSE. He slept under BRIDGES and on PARK BENCHES. Wicked Wilf is no stranger to Woodford PRISON either where the violent villain was once locked up for a WHOLE YEAR.'

'Is this true, Wilf?' Barney asked.

Wilf was staring at his shoes. 'Sort of. I was in jail, but only for a month, not for a whole year. I punched a fellow on the nose. He said something horrible about my mum. It was a long time ago.'

'No, no, I don't mean about your being in jail. Is it true that before you came to live with me you had no home?'

Wilf looked up, surprised. 'Yes,' he said.

'And did you really sleep under bridges and on park benches?'

'I did.'

'That must have been awful.'

'Yes Barney, it was horrible.'

'So if you left me, where would you go?'

Wilf scratched his nose. 'Dunno. Back to the park, I suppose. Or down to the river.'

'How can you think of leaving me then? How can you even think of it?'

'I was sure you'd throw me out as soon as you saw the newspaper.'

'This is your home now,' Barney said firmly, even sternly, which surprised Wilf for he was usually so timid and hesitant.

'I really was in jail,' Wilf reminded him.

'It was a long time ago,' said Barney.

'I did punch someone. It's true, you know.'

'He said something horrible about your mum,' replied Barney, and he added, 'Let me hear no more talk of leaving. Now tell me, what are you planning for lunch?'

And that was the end of that.

Two days later, Barney was out for a walk when he saw a little cat playing with some dandelions, patting their fluffy heads with her paw and then watching the seeds float off into the sky.

'Puss puss!' he called to her.

The cat mewed, ran over to him, and started to rub against his ankles. Barney bent down and picked her up. She was a small thin cat and she was cold. 'Poor little thing,' he said. 'Poor little Dandelion cat.' He put her into the front of his cardigan to keep her warm, and fastened the buttons up so that her face peeped out above them. The cat started to purr and Barney could feel the heat of her fur now against his tummy. 'Let's go home, shall we?' he said. 'Let's go and have something to eat.'

And from that day on the cat was called Dandelion and she was Barney's cat.

Now when Wilf brought the trolley in the morning with Barney's breakfast, he brought Dandelion's too, on the lower shelf. After about a week, Wilf came in one morning looking grim. 'It's your turn this time, Pussens,' and he nodded at the newspaper as he held it out to Barney.

'Oh dear,' said Barney. 'I suppose we'd better get it over with and see what they're saying this time.'

On the front of the paper in large print it said: 'MAD MILLIONAIRE IN STRAY CAT SHOCK! Full story and SENSATIONAL picture on page 7!'

'I'll read it aloud,' Barney said. He knew the cat couldn't read but he was too polite to say so.

'Mad Millionaire Barney Barrington has done it AGAIN! The *Woodford Trumpet* can reveal today that he is now sharing his HOME with a black and white ALLEY CAT called Dandelion. Too MEAN to buy himself a BEAUTIFUL EXPENSIVE cat with LONG soft fur and BIG blue eyes, Barmy Barney has chosen instead a MISERABLE little stray with SHORT fur and THIN whiskers. Dandelion is seen above in our exclusive shock photo LICKING HER OWN BUM!'

And sure enough, there at the top of the page was a big picture of Dandelion sitting in the garden, with her back leg in the air and her head down, having a jolly good lick. She went pink under her fur when she saw it. She hadn't thought that anyone was watching her and she certainly hadn't thought that anyone was taking photographs. Barney had never seen a cat blush before but he pretended not to notice.

'Poor little Dandelion,' he murmured, tickling her behind the ear. 'Pay no heed. Everybody'll have forgotten about it by tomorrow. Put it out of your mind.'

'Yes, Barney's right,' Wilf said, and then he added, 'All it means is that you're one of us now.'

Sitting on Barney's plate was his morning post. There was only one letter today and he opened it as Wilf poured the coffee. It was from the bank.

Dear Mr Barrington,
Please find enclosed your annual bank statement. I am sure you will be delighted to see how much your money has grown during the past year. As I was sending it I wanted to put in a note to say how very happy, in fact how completely thrilled we are to deal with someone who ~~has such a lot of money~~ is such a nice person.
Yours oh so very sincerely, dear Mr Barrington,
Sylvester Simkins
Bank Manager

'What a creep!' Wilf said.

Barney took the bank statement out of the envelope and unfolded it. And unfolded it and unfolded it and unfolded it. It was a huge sheet of paper: it had to be so that there would be room for all the noughts. 'Goodness me, as much as that!' Barney said, looking at the figure at the bottom of the page.

'I would start to spend some of that if I was you,' Wilf said. 'I know what! Why don't you buy yourself a BEAUTIFUL EXPENSIVE cat with LONG soft fur and BIG blue eyes. Only joking, Pussens,' he added as Dandelion looked up, worried. 'Anyway, I'm off. Enjoy your breakfast. You're getting an omelette for your lunch today and the cat's getting a kipper. I'll bring it up at one o'clock. If you need anything else before then, give me a shout.'

It was lovely living with Wilf, Barney thought after he'd gone. He was so direct, you always knew exactly where you stood.

JASPER'S JOB

There was nothing Jasper liked more than money. He thought about it all the time and no matter how much of it he had, still he wanted more. If you had crept into his bedroom in the middle of the night when he was fast asleep and lifted up his eyelid, you would have seen a little pound sign there, as Jasper dreamt about coins and bank notes and gold.

Nobody knew how he made his money. When people asked him what he did he would look them in the eye and say, 'Actually, I'm a specialist in the area of material supplies concerning international conflict.'

Of course nobody had the foggiest notion what he meant by this. However, because people don't like to admit not knowing things in case it makes them look foolish, they pretended they did.

'Are you really?' people would reply. 'My

goodness, how interesting.'

Sometimes Jasper would even say, 'You do know what I mean by the area of material supplies concerning international conflict, don't you?'

'Of course! Of course!' they cried.

And by this Jasper knew for sure that they didn't.

The day Dandelion's photograph was in the newspaper was to be a busy one for Jasper. He hated getting up early and so he was in a foul temper at breakfast, even worse than usual. 'You didn't put my milk on my cornflakes for me!' he shouted at his maid.

'I thought it best to wait,' she said. 'I thought they would get all soggy on the way up from the kitchen.'

'They're nice like that!' Jasper bellowed. 'I like 'em soggy! Don't you even know that by now?'

But the woman didn't know because she had only been working for him for a week, and there were so many things he did and didn't like that it was impossible to remember them all in such a short time. The toast had to be buttered while it was still hot. The milk had to go into the cup before the tea. All the crusts had to be cut off the bread before it got to the table because he hated crusts. Jasper had a million little whims and when he didn't get exactly what he wanted he went wild. It took about two months to learn all his ways, but by that stage the servants had usually had enough. Some of them gave in their notice, but some of them were so afraid of him they simply climbed out of the window in the night and ran away.

Cannibal and Bruiser did nothing to stop them. 'Lucky thing,' they thought wistfully as they watched the latest maid or butler or valet climb over the gates at midnight and race off up the street to freedom. 'Wish it was us.'

Breakfast over, Jasper hopped out of bed and put on a sharp pinstriped suit, and slapped lashings of *eau de cologne* around his chops. It smelt quite delightfully of lemons and pinecones. Jasper had it specially made, for him alone, at mind-boggling expense. In the car on the way to the factory this morning he remembered that the head groundsman, whose job it was to feed the dogs, had done a bunk the day before and Jasper had forgotten to tell any of the other members of staff to look after the animals. 'None of them will think of it,' he said to himself. 'They're all too stupid. Oh well, Cannibal and Bruiser are big lads. I'm sure they can look out for themselves.'

The factory was buried deep in the heart of the dark forest at the edge of the town and was surrounded by a series of high fences, each one topped with coils of razor wire. At each of three different gates Jasper had to give a password and show a special card with his photograph on it, to prove that he was who he said he was. At last his car rumbled to a halt in front of the dark windowless façade of the factory. Even Jasper had to admit it looked a bit sinister.

A glum-looking man was slumped in a little cabin at the front door. 'Tell Mr Smith I'm here to see him,' Jasper said briskly.

'He expecting you?'

'You know as well as I do Mr Smith sees no one unless they make an appointment.'

'Trick question,' said the glum-looking man. He made a brief telephone call and in no time at all Jasper was sitting in Mr Smith's office.

Mr Smith was as ordinary looking and unremarkable as his name suggested (although it was rumoured that Mr Smith wasn't his real name). He wore a grey suit with a neat white shirt and a blue tie. The only unusual thing about him was that he had a little gold tooth that could be seen when he smiled (which he didn't often do). He and Jasper greeted each other warmly. 'How's business?' Jasper said.

'Excellent, oh excellent,' exclaimed Mr Smith. 'We have some wonderful new products that I'm sure you'll be very excited about. Let's begin shall we?'

From the drawer of his desk he took a little thing no bigger than a hazelnut. It was olive green and he set it in the palm of Jasper's hand so that he could inspect it.

'This is our latest invention,' he said. 'It's a hand grenade. A hundred times smaller than a conventional grenade, but every bit as powerful. It means that soldiers can carry more of them into battle.'

'Gosh, that's clever!' Jasper said. 'What genius thought that one up?'

'Me, actually,' said Mr Smith. He blushed modestly and gave one of his rare smiles, showing for a moment his little gold tooth. 'It was my idea but the boys in the backroom have been working for years now to make it a reality.'

'Wonderful!' Jasper said. 'How much are they?' Mr Smith named his price. 'I'll take four hundred to begin with.'

'Knew you'd like 'em.' Mr Smith took an invoice form from his desk and started to fill it in. He offered all kinds of guns and bombs, landmines and rockets and explosives to Jasper, who placed his order, saying that he would take the grenades with him, and that everything else could be delivered at a later date.

'A pleasure to do business with you, as always,' Mr Smith said, showing his little gold tooth again briefly as he carefully poured the hand grenades into the open maw of Jasper's black leather briefcase.

From the factory, Jasper drove straight to the airport. At the top of the flight of steps leading into his plane a stewardess was standing smiling at the passengers. She stopped smiling when she recognised Jasper. 'Hello Gorgeous,' he said, smacking her hard on the bum as he passed. 'Hope you've got loads of nice grub on board today or I'll want to know the reason why.' He was laughing as he said it but it was a strange, unfunny sort of laugh. The stewardess shivered.

By the time he arrived at his destination he was burping and farting from all the free champagne he had drunk during the flight.

'Good riddance,' murmured the stewardess as he went down the steps of the plane.

Jasper jumped into a taxi. 'Take me to The Villa,' said.

The Villa was a big pink house on the edge of the city, and when he arrived there he found it surrounded by police and security men, trying to hold back a huge crowd of journalists and cameramen and photographers.

Jasper paid them no heed and went round to the back, where he found a hole in the fence. Slipping through, he hurried across the gardens towards The Villa itself, crept up to a window and peeped in.

The room Jasper saw was a grand one, with a high painted ceiling, crystal chandeliers and many mirrors. Two angry-looking men sat opposite each other at a big shiny table. One of them wore a military uniform with oodles of gold braid on his hat, his shoulders and his chest. The other was a middle-aged man in a grey suit who looked rather like Mr Smith except that he had no gold tooth. Between them sat an anxious-looking woman, wringing her hands. Suddenly, the man in the suit banged the table hard with his fists and jumped up.

'Our lot are going to kill your lot!' he shouted.

The man in the uniform banged his fists on the table and jumped up too. 'Just you try it!' he roared. 'Just you try it!'

The two men were now eyeball to eyeball, glaring at each other.

'Gentlemen, please, this is getting us nowhere,' said the anxious woman in the middle. She turned to the man in the uniform, 'General, please calm yourself.' And to the man in the suit, 'Mr President, I ask you, please don't shout like that. I think we ought to break now and have a cup of tea and a rest. We can meet again in an hour and by that time I hope your tempers will have cooled.'

Dragging their feet and scowling, The President and The General left the room. Jasper, whom no one had noticed, melted away from the window.

About twenty minutes later, he came upon The General sitting alone on a bench in the garden in a deep sulk. 'I heard all that,' Jasper said softly, sidling up to him. 'I heard what he said to you, that other man. I wouldn't put up with it if I were you.'

The General turned to look at him. 'Who are you?' he asked. 'What are you doing here?'

'I'm a specialist,' Jasper said, 'in the area of material supplies concerning international conflict.'

'Are you?' said The General. 'Are you indeed?'

And unlike most people Jasper knew, he clearly understood exactly what was meant by this.

From his pocket Jasper took one of the tiny grenades he had got from Mr Smith and held it out on the palm of his hand. He explained what it was to The General, who was very impressed. 'How much do they cost?'

Jasper named his price, which was five times what he had paid Mr Smith, adding, 'I can let you have two hundred of them here and now, and I can get you loads of other stuff too: guns, explosives, anything you want.'

'Done deal,' said The General, who placed his order, paid Jasper and went off happy with his bag of grenades.

But what would The General have said had he known that five minutes after they parted, Jasper was sitting on a bench elsewhere in the garden with The President, having exactly the same conversation and selling him the other two hundred grenades?

As The General and The President went back into The Villa to meet again, Jasper slipped out through the hole in the fence and hailed a passing taxi. 'Take me to the airport.' As he was going up the steps of the plane, already he could hear the first explosions.

Tired after his long day, he slept the whole way home. All the stewardesses were pleased about this, because although he was snoring so loudly you could hear him even over the engines of the plane, it was still better than having him awake and pestering them all the time.

Night had fallen by the time he got back to his own country, and by now he was grumpy. 'Everything all right?' he asked the butler when he arrived back at the house.

'Not really, Sir,' the butler said. 'The butcher came round with a big bill for some steaks Cannibal and Bruiser stole from his shop this afternoon.'

'If he thinks I'm going to pay he can think

again. He should look after his meat, not leave it lying around where the dogs can get at it.'

By the time the maid brought his cocoa up to his room, Jasper was already in his blue and white striped pyjamas and tucked up in bed. It was the same maid who had brought him his cornflakes that morning and she was exhausted because she had been working hard all day. While Jasper was sitting in the plane drinking champagne she had been beating carpets and scrubbing floors.

'And what,' he said, pointing to three biscuits beside his cup, 'are those things?'

'Biscuits, Sir. Chocolate fingers.'

'I can see that,' Jasper thundered. 'I'm not stupid, woman. But don't you know that I only ever have chocolate fingers with my afternoon tea? I have to have malted milk biscuits with my cocoa every night, pink wafers with my elevenses and jammy dodgers after my lunch except for Saturdays, when I have jaffa cakes. Have you got that?'

'I think so.'

'HAVE YOU GOT THAT?!!!'

'Yes Sir. Sorry Sir.' The woman was trying hard not to cry. 'I suppose,' she thought to herself, 'I could simply climb out of the window in the middle of the night and run away.'

After she had left the room Jasper drank his cocoa and ate his biscuits, even if they *were* chocolate fingers. Then he turned on the radio. 'Good evening. Here is the news. Reports are coming in that a horrible war has broken out between...'

'Oh snakes' elbows! Who cares!' Jasper said crossly, and he turned the radio off again. He switched the light out and curled up in his bed.

And within five minutes Jasper was fast asleep, dreaming about money, about coins and bank notes and gold.

BARNEY AT HOME

Even though his house was enormous, Barney lived in only one room, on the top floor at the extreme right of the building. 'Why did you buy such a big place?' Wilf asked him.

'The man in the estate agent's told me it was all they had left.'

'They saw you coming,' said Wilf, shaking his head. He now lived in a room beside the kitchen on the ground floor, at the extreme left of the building. The first time he saw Barney's room he had thought it very odd, the strangest place he had ever seen in his whole life. And in truth, it was an unusual room.

Just under the window was Barney's little bed. Beside it was the wicker basket in which Dandelion slept (although it was not unknown for her to climb out of this in the middle of the night and snuggle in beside Barney until morning came). There was the table and chair at which Barney ate his meals (although it was not unknown for Wilf to eat with him and so there was an extra chair). There was the cosy sofa on which he sat to listen to music or to read, for there was also a bookcase crammed with good books. On the wall was the painting of the lady with a yellow butterfly balanced on the tip of her finger. There was a miniature tree growing in a shallow pot. But what made the room remarkable was that slap bang in the middle of it, taking up all the spare space, was a huge black grand piano with its lid propped open. Even though he no longer gave concerts, Barney still spent hours and hours every day playing the piano. It was his greatest happiness in life.

Every afternoon now at half past four, Barney and Wilf had milk and cherry buns together and talked about things.

'Why don't you put the piano in another room?' Wilf asked one day as he poured the milk.

'I like to be near it all the time,' Barney said. If he woke in the night, it comforted him to see the piano looming there in the darkness.

'And the little tree: where did you get that?'

'A lady in Japan gave it to me.'

He told Wilf that the lady's name was O-Haru. She wrote poems using a brush and ink rather than a pen. She grew miniature trees, Barney said, she had a whole perfect forest of them. In the autumn their leaves turned gold and yellow and red. In the springtime tiny buds appeared, then tiny leaves and blossoms. O-Haru lived in a house with paper walls and had a garden in which there were no flowers, only stones and fine raked sand.

Wilf, who had never been out of Woodford in his life, listened to all of this with astonishment. Some of the things Barney spoke of were so extraordinary that at first Wilf wondered if he was making it all up, just to tease him. But then as he got to know him better he realised that Barney would never do such a thing.

'Were you always as shy as you are now?' Wilf asked. 'Were you one of those little boys who wouldn't sing a song at a party unless you were hiding behind the door so that no one would know it was you, even if they did know because they saw you going behind the door in the first place?'

'Yes.'

'Then how did you manage to give all those concerts in front of hundreds and thousands of people?'

'Oh it was awful, Wilf!' Barney exclaimed. 'I can't tell you how terrible it was, at least to begin with.'

He went on to describe how scared he used to be when he was little, standing in the wings in his best suit waiting to go on. He could sense the audience out there on the far side of the footlights, snuffling and whispering like a thousand-headed monster. Barney knew that as soon as he put his toes on the stage everyone would start to clap their hands and he hated that too. The noise frightened him. Out there in the middle of the stage in a pool of bright light he could see his beloved piano. He knew that if only he could get to it and start to play, then everything would be all right. He would be happy and feel safe. But getting from the wings to the piano was like walking along the edge of a high cliff, with an angry sea crashing on the rocks below and thinking that at any moment you might fall in.

'But then,' he went on, 'my mother found a

magic curtain. Every night before a concert she hung it up at the edge of the stage. It was invisible, but I knew it was there. It meant that I could see the audience, but they couldn't see me. I felt that I was completely on my own and so walking over to my piano wasn't a problem.'

'Do you still have the curtain?' Wilf asked, and Barney gave a strange little smile.

'No,' he said. 'I grew up and then I grew old and my mother wasn't there any more. But by then I understood how the magic curtain worked. I didn't need it any longer. I was able to walk across the stage alone. But I always loved the end of a concert.'

'Because it was over?'

'Because I knew I'd made the people happy,' Barney said. 'When I heard the applause at the end, I knew that I'd given them something special, something wonderful that they would remember for the rest of their lives. And that made me very happy.'

'You're still very shy,' Wilf remarked.

'Yes,' said Barney, 'I suppose I am. But O-Haru is even shyer.'

Wilf imagined them sitting side by side, silent

and blushing but completely happy in a forest of miniature trees, or in a garden in which there were no flowers, only stones and fine raked sand.

Later the same day, as darkness fell, it began to rain. A man on his way home from work stood in under a chestnut tree opposite Barney's house to take shelter. As he waited there, he noticed that in all of the great house only two lights were lit, one on the top floor at the extreme right of the building and one on the ground floor at the extreme left.

Just at that moment a young woman appeared beside him. 'Has it started yet?' she asked, peering anxiously at the house from under her dripping umbrella.

'Has what started?'

'The lights,' she said. 'The switching on of the lights. Look, look, it's beginning now!'

As she spoke, the window to the left of the one at the top right of the house also lit up and then the window to the left again, and then the one beside that. Slowly the yellow light seemed to flow along the whole of the top floor of the building in a steady wave from right to left, until all the windows were lit. 'It happens at this time every night,' the woman said breathlessly. 'I always try to get here in time to see it because it's such a beautiful thing.'

The man agreed. There was something mysterious and fascinating in what was happening. By now a window had been lit up on the extreme left of the floor below the one that was already completely illuminated, and now the yellow light was again flowing steadily, only this time left to right.

'They say he's weird, and I read in the *Woodford Trumpet* that he's very mean.'

The young woman shrugged. 'You can't believe everything it says in the papers.'

Now the light was flowing along a third floor. They stood watching in silence until finally it reached the last window in the house, on the extreme left on the ground floor, the window that had been lit up all along. The whole huge house was now ablaze with light against the darkening sky. 'It is beautiful,' the man admitted.

'It's magnificent.'

'It looks like an ocean liner,' he said, 'out at

sea in the middle of the night.'

But the woman said that it reminded her of that moment at a party when all the lights have been put out and the birthday cake is carried into the blackness of the room. 'And all the small soft flames flicker on the candles and then everyone begins to sing.'

The house remained lit up for some ten or fifteen minutes and the woman and man stood there in the shadow of the great tree, simply looking at it. And then all of a sudden, the light in the extreme bottom left-hand window went out. Then the light in the window beside that was also extinguished, and then the window beside that. Now it was darkness rather than light that was flowing along from one window to the next, and as it did the house seemed to disappear from the bottom up.

'How strange it is,' the woman said softly. 'How strange and how lovely.'

Only the top floor of the house was lit now and gradually darkness overcame that too, in a wave from left to right. Eventually a light was burning in only one window of the great house: the window on the extreme right of the top floor of the building. It remained lit for some five or ten minutes and when all of a sudden it went out, the whole building disappeared.

'And you say this happens every night?' the man asked the woman.

'Every night,' she replied. 'Sometimes, like tonight, it happens very smoothly. Then on other occasions the light might suddenly stop flowing for ten minutes or more before beginning again.'

'Why?'

The woman shook her head. 'I have no idea,' she said, 'absolutely no idea whatsoever. It's all a complete mystery.'

Suddenly the man and woman realised that they were standing there in the darkness together under the woman's umbrella.

'I suppose I'd best be off,' said the man.

'Me too.'

'Goodnight then.'

'Goodnight.'

Even though they didn't know each other it had been wonderful to watch the strange light show in each other's company. They felt shy and they blushed but they were completely happy too, like Barney and O-Haru in the miniature forest or the garden where there were no flowers, only stones and fine raked sand.

THE PAINTING

What on earth was Barney doing?

As with so many things that seem completely mysterious, the explanation was really quite simple. At the exact moment when the young woman with the umbrella arrived at the chestnut tree, Barney turned to Dandelion who was curled up snoozing under the piano. 'Come along, Puss,' he said. 'It's time to go.'

With the cat at his heels he stepped out of the bedroom and switched on the light. Before Barney was a long dim corridor. All along the left-hand side were windows, and all along the right-hand side hung a series of marvellous paintings. The first showed a handsome man in a dark red robe and a velvet hat.

'Good evening, young Sir,' Barney murmured as he passed by and switched on the second light. This revealed the second painting, of a bowl of wood strawberries on a crisp white linen cloth. Barney paused briefly to admire it. The strawberries were so lifelike that he could almost taste them in his mouth. He switched on the next light and smiled. 'You like this one, don't you,' he said to Dandelion.

The cat mewed and put her paws up on the wall, trying to touch the painting of a fine fat silver salmon lying on a china plate.

Barney plodded steadily onwards, switching on light after light as he went on looking at all his paintings. At the end of the corridor was a short spiral staircase which he carefully descended, bringing him onto a similar passageway, although now the windows were on his right-hand side and the paintings on his left. *Click, click, click* went the light switches. *Clump, clump, clump* went Barney's feet. Dandelion's soft paws made no sound at all. Slowly they made their way through the house until they were on the ground floor.

At the end of the final corridor was a stout door on which Barney knocked.

'Come in, come in.' Wilf was standing by the stove in his slippers and dressing gown, his eyes bright and his hair on end. As soon as Barney came into the room Wilf set a pan on the stove to heat, then bent down and poured out a saucer of milk for Dandelion. 'There you go, Pussens, there's your supper.' As the cat drank, Wilf pottered around the kitchen preparing two mugs of cocoa and chatting to Barney about the day that was ending.

'Thank you for helping me with everything and looking after me so well,' Barney said.

'My pleasure. There you go. Mind now, it's hot.'

'Thank you, Wilf. Sleep well.'

'You too, Barney. Have nice dreams. Night night, Pussens.'

With Dandelion licking the milk from her whiskers and Barney carrying his mug of hot cocoa, they set out to retrace their steps through the house. Barney switched off each of the lights in turn as they went and said a last goodnight to his paintings. By the time he reached the bedroom his cocoa had cooled enough for him to drink it. Then he said goodnight to Dandelion, turned out the light and in no time at all Barney was fast asleep.

The following morning, Wilf soft-boiled two eggs for Barney's breakfast and grilled a mackerel for Dandelion. He brought the food upstairs on the trolley as usual. 'There's something in the paper this morning that you'll find interesting,' he said.

On the front of the *Woodford Trumpet* was a photograph of Barney out cycling. He was freewheeling down a hill on his bike with his hair on end so that it looked even wilder than Wilf's. Dandelion's face peeked out above the middle button of his cardigan, for he often carried her around like this now, as he had done on the day he found her.

'BARMY BARNEY GETS ON HIS BIKE!' said the caption below the photograph.

'To be honest, that sort of thing doesn't interest me,' Barney said, carefully tapping at the top of his boiled egg. 'It doesn't even bother me any more. It's just silliness.'

'No, no, I didn't mean that. Look here, at the top of the page,' and Wilf pointed to the headline 'ANGEL GOES UP FOR SALE.'

'That's just silliness too,' Barney said, glancing at the paper again as he put salt on his egg. 'Everybody knows you can't buy an angel and even if you could, what would you do with it?'

'Oh just read it will you!' exclaimed Wilf, who was beginning to lose patience.

'Sorry,' said Barney and putting down his egg spoon he obediently picked up the newspaper. 'The Haverford-Snuffley Angel is up for sale. The Haverford-Snuffley Angel! My goodness, why didn't you say so? This does interest me, Wilf. It interests me very much indeed.'

Surprisingly enough it interested Jasper too. At that very moment he was also sitting up in bed reading the paper and eating soft-boiled eggs. (It was a Tuesday.) 'Listen to this, lads,' he said to Cannibal and Bruiser, who were still snoozing in their basket.

Barney and Jasper began to read aloud the same piece from the paper at exactly the same moment.

'The Haverford-Snuffley Angel is up for sale. "It's a TINY little painting, no bigger than a POSTCARD," Mrs Haverford-Snuffley told our reporter yesterday in an EXCLUSIVE interview with the *Woodford Trumpet*. "It's been in our family for HUNDREDS and HUNDREDS of years, ever since it was PAINTED for Theophilus Haverford-Snuffley. I don't WANT to sell it now but I HAVE TO because I need the MONEY. Haverford-Snuffley Hall is FALLING DOWN. There's a great big HOLE in the roof. I have a

JAM-JAR at the bottom of my BED to catch the rain and I'm FED UP with having to rise in the middle of the NIGHT to empty it. It's freezing cold in ALL the rooms because there's a great big HOLE in the FRONT DOOR too. Then last month we discovered heaps of BATS living in the ATTIC and even they were cold and damp and SHIVERING. Although the Haverford-Snuffley Angel is a TINY painting I expect to SELL it for POTS and POTS of money. So I'll be able to FIX the front DOOR and the hole in the ROOF and make the ATTIC nice and COMFY for the BATS. Who knows, I might even have enough LEFT OVER to buy myself a NEW HAT!" The Haverford-Snuffley Angel will be sold by SPECIAL AUCTION in the Woodford Sale Room next FRIDAY at 1.00pm sharp.'

'The size of a postcard,' Jasper said, nibbling thoughtfully on a toast soldier. 'You don't get a lot of angel for your money, do you?'

'I saw it once you know, Wilf,' Barney said. 'Mrs Haverford-Snuffley loaned it to an exhibition and I saw it there. It was one of the loveliest things I've ever seen in my whole life.' His boiled eggs were going cold in front of him. 'Just think, if you owned it you could look at it every single day in the year. How marvellous that would be!'

'If you owned it you could close it away, and then nobody would ever be able to see it,' said Jasper, licking butter off his fingers. 'Even if it cost lots of money now, you could probably sell it for lots more in the future. And everybody would be dead impressed that you were rich enough to spend all that money on a piddling little painting.'

And once again Barney and Jasper, without knowing it, suddenly spoke aloud together, saying exactly the same thing in exactly the same moment: 'I simply have to have it!'

THE AUCTION

The whole of Woodford was abuzz and agog when Friday came. A great crowd of people pressed into the sale room at half past twelve and jostled for the best seats. The reporter from the *Woodford Trumpet* was scampering around talking to people and scribbling furiously in his notebook the whole time. The photographer was there too, taking pictures of everyone as they arrived.

Plooff! Here was Jasper Jellit looking elegant in a white linen suit, with Cannibal and Bruiser on two stout leather leads.

Plooff! Here was Mrs Haverford-Snuffley wearing a straw hat with a hole in the crown and a bat hanging from the brim. 'We're both terribly excited, aren't we?' she said and the bat nodded. 'I want a new front door and all the bats want central heating.'

Plooff! Here was Philomena Phelan, the

director of the Woodford Art Gallery, with a glum expression on her face. 'We'd love to buy the painting for the gallery so that everyone in the town could see it whenever they wanted,' she said, 'but we have hardly any money so I'm not very hopeful.'

Plooff! Here was a strange-looking character who crept into the room and didn't want to have his photograph taken at all. He was wearing dark glasses that may well have hidden a pair of small bright eyes, and although his hair was plastered flat to his head that might only have been because he had put wax on it: usually, it probably stood straight up in mad tufts. The pink nose of a cat poked out from the pocket of his jacket.

Up at the front of the room was the Haverford-Snuffley Angel, displayed for all to see. Although it really was no bigger than a postcard it was bright as a jewel. The angel had soft brown hair and eyes like a squirrel. Its wings were made of coloured feathers, crimson and green and deep, deep blue. It wore a simple linen gown and in its hands it held a strange musical instrument, like a violin with only one string. The angel looked as if it was alive.

Small wooden paddles were being given out to the people who were seriously interested in buying the painting. Jasper and Philomena took one each, as did the mysterious stranger. He then took a mobile phone out of his pocket. 'Hello? That you? It's me, Wilf,' he whispered into it. 'Listen, I'm really nervous. Explain to me again how the whole thing works.'

'Have you got your paddle?' Barney said.

'Yes.'

'Well, the man will say a price and if you're willing to pay that price, you lift your paddle. The auctioneer then says a new, higher price. If someone else is willing to pay that, they hold up their paddle. It goes on like this until the price the auctioneer says is so high that no one wants to pay it. The last person who had their paddle up when the man bangs the desk with his hammer gets to buy the painting,' said Barney, who was hopeless at explaining difficult things. 'Do you understand?'

'Oo-er, I'm not sure that I do,' Wilf said.

'Don't worry, you'll see how it works once the bidding starts. I'm going to stay on the line, so I'll help you if I can. Just do your best.'

Everybody was settling down in their seats now, for the auction was about to begin. At exactly one o'clock, an important-looking man in a dark suit swept into the room. He went up to a desk at the front beside the painting and taking out a small wooden hammer he knocked *rat-a-tat* three times. 'Ladies and gentlemen, welcome. We only have one item for sale today, but it is a remarkable one: the world-famous Haverford-Snuffley Angel. And so without further ado, let me open the bidding at five thousand.' Philomena Phelan eagerly lifted her paddle.

'Six thousand.' Jasper lifted his.

'Seven thousand.' Philomena lifted hers again.

'Eight thousand.' Once more Jasper.

'Ouch!' Wilf suddenly felt a set of sharp claws jab him in the stomach. Looking down, he saw a cross little cat's face glaring at him from under the flap of his jacket pocket. 'Gosh, yes, I'd better start bidding too,' he thought.

'Nine thousand.' Wilf lifted his paddle and the auctioneer nodded towards him.

'Ten thousand.' Philomena Phelan again.

The bidding went on like this for quite some time. It struck Wilf that perhaps they had started with a ridiculously low price so that they would all have a chance to get used to waving their paddles in the air and stop feeling nervous.

'How are we doing?' said Barney's voice in the phone that Wilf had kept pressed to his ear all this time.

'I think I'm getting the hang of it,' Wilf hissed back.

By now the price had gone up to seventy thousand and Philomena Phelan was beginning to look worried but she lifted her paddle all the same. 'Eighty thousand.' Jasper proudly raised his paddle.

'Ninety thousand,' said the auctioneer. Wilf made his bid.

Looking sad and disappointed Philomena put her paddle down. She was going to have to stop bidding: the Haverford-Snuffley Angel was too expensive to buy for the people of Woodford.

Now it was all down to Jasper and Wilf! Which of them would hold his nerve and win the day?

'One hundred thousand.' Jasper lifted his paddle and smiled at the auctioneer. Afterwards, some people would say that they thought they also saw Cannibal and Bruiser grinning from time to time during the auction. One woman even claimed she saw them wink at each other but she must have imagined it, for such a thing isn't possible.

'It's getting very dear,' Wilf whispered into the phone. 'It's up to one hundred thousand.'

'That's all right, I can manage that,' Barney replied. But it was a lot of money for a painting, and the people in the room were beginning to be astonished at how high the price was going.

'Two hundred thousand!' Wilf again.

'Three hundred thousand!' Jasper waved his paddle.

'Oooohhh!' said the crowd, as though it were at a circus.

'Four hundred thousand!'

'Aaaaahhh!'

'Five hundred thousand!'

'Goodness me! You bats will get your central heating, that's for sure,' cried Mrs Haverford-Snuffley.

'Six hundred thousand!' The crowd gave a strangled gasp with a kind of giggle somewhere in the middle of it, as Wilf raised his paddle and made his bid.

'This is a world record for a painting of this

size,' said the auctioneer who had gone pink in the face. He was terribly excited but he was trying not to show it.

'Seven hundred thousand!' Jasper again!

'We're getting close to my limit, Wilf,' Barney said. 'If it gets much more expensive than this, I can't afford it.'

'Eight hundred thousand!' Dandelion put her paws over her ears as Wilf lifted his paddle. The suspense was too much; she couldn't bear to listen.

'Nine hundred thousand!' Jasper!

'We can go to a million but no higher,' Barney said.

'One million!' cried the auctioneer and Wilf waved his paddle in the air.

'One million I am bid! Do I hear one million one hundred thousand?'

All eyes were on Jasper now, and he knew it. He was at his limit too, but he wasn't going to stop. Everyone was holding their breath, waiting to see if he would bid one million one hundred thousand. He twiddled the paddle as if he could hardly be bothered to lift it, as if the whole thing had become a bore to him. But he was within a whisker of getting what he wanted. All he had to do was raise his hand and the Haverford-Snuffley Angel would be his. Pretending to yawn, he moved to lift the paddle and make the final bid for one million one hundred thousand.

But before he could do it, just at that very moment, to everyone's amazement something completely unexpected happened. Cannibal jumped up and grabbed Jasper's wooden paddle, snapping it in two. In exactly the same moment Bruiser leapt and sent Jasper flying, knocking him backwards off his chair and on to the floor. 'Eeek! Gerroff!' he cried, for Bruiser was sitting on his chest now, growling and pinning him down.

'One million one hundred thousand! No takers?' shouted the auctioneer over the racket, for the place was in uproar. Mrs Haverford-Snuffley fainted and the bat fluttered wildly around the room. The reporter from the *Woodford Trumpet* couldn't write fast enough to keep up with everything that was happening, and the photographer was taking pictures non-stop. *Plooff! Plooff!*

Cannibal was smashing the paddle into matchsticks and Bruiser was still sitting on top of Jasper growling. People shrieked and Dandelion popped out of Wilf's pocket and climbed onto his head, the better to see what was happening.

'Do I hear any advance on one million?' It was still Wilf's bid!

'Miaow!'

'Stoppit! Down boy!'

'Going for one million!'

'Aaargh!'

Plooff!

'Gggrrrrhh!'

'Help!'

'Going!' shouted the auctioneer at the top of his voice over all the hullabaloo. 'Going, going…' and he banged on the desk with his hammer… 'GONE!

'Gone for one million to the little fat man with a mobile phone and a cat on his head!'

THE NEXT DAY

Worn out with all the excitement, Mrs Haverford-Snuffley spent the whole of the following morning in bed, fanned from time to time by the cooling wings of an obliging bat. On the faded wallpaper was a bright rectangle, no bigger than a postcard, where the Haverford-Snuffley Angel had hung for so many years.

Over at The Oaks, Wilf was shattered. He awoke with a groan and looked around the room. To the left, propped against his alarm clock, was the Haverford-Snuffley Angel itself. To the right, standing beside the bed and holding a silver tray, was Barney. 'Good morning Wilf. *I've* brought *you* your breakfast this morning!'

On the tray was a clean white linen cloth and a pot of hot chocolate. There were pats of butter, raspberry jam and a china dish of Woodford

Creams, one of Wilf's most favourite things. He lifted back the cloth on the bread basket and took out a crisp roll.

'It's still warm!'

'They're freshly baked,' Barney said. 'They were hot from the oven when I bought them and I hurried home.'

'You went to the bakery?!'

'I did, yes.'

Wilf could hardly believe his ears. Barney never went shopping: never EVER.

'I just stood in the queue with everyone else and I did feel shy,' he admitted. 'I thought everyone was looking at me.'

'They weren't, you know,' Wilf said. 'They were looking at the bread and cakes. They didn't give a hoot about you. They were too busy trying to make up their minds about whether they would have a Danish pastry or an apple turnover.'

'Perhaps they were,' Barney said and he smiled timidly. 'When my turn came and the woman behind the counter asked what I wanted, I felt like running away. But I knew that if I did, you wouldn't have any fresh bread for your breakfast. And you probably wanted to run away from the auction yesterday but then I wouldn't have got to buy the painting.'

'Too right,' said Wilf, turning to look at the Angel again. It was proof that it had all really happened, that it wasn't just some wild dream he had had. 'We did it though, didn't we?' he said. Turning back, he grinned at Barney as he popped a Woodford Cream in his mouth.

'We did it!'

And as for Jasper...

'I've brought you your breakfast, Sir.'

'Don't want it.'

'It's rice crispies.'

'Don't want them.'

'They're nice and soggy, just the way you like them.'

'GO AWAY!'

Jasper was in a massive sulk, lying in bed with the blankets pulled up over his head. Even after the maid left the room he stayed like that for quite some time until he ran out of air. Then he poked his head out and stared at the ceiling, trying to remember the last time he'd wanted something and hadn't got it. Eventually he decided it must have been when he was six and had his heart set on a pet crocodile but his mother said no.

What had come over Cannibal and Bruiser yesterday, he wondered, curling up and starting to suck the end of the quilt to comfort himself. It was almost as if they'd had a plan, as if they'd dreamed up together what they would do even before they arrived at the sale room. It never crossed his mind that it might have had something to do with the chocolate party some weeks earlier.

Suddenly he noticed that the maid had left a copy of the *Woodford Trumpet* on the bedside table. He gave a low moan and slid back under the blankets again. Ten minutes later a hand emerged and picked up the newspaper, taking it back in under the heaped-up bedding.

The *Woodford Trumpet* did not make happy reading for Jasper that morning and the photographs were no consolation. Usually Jasper loved to have his picture in the paper, but not when it showed him cowering under one of his own dogs. 'MAD MUTTS MAKE MAYHEM AS ANGEL GOES FOR A MILLION!' read the main headline. There were long reports about how there had almost been a RIOT at the auction, how a BAT had FAINTED and how the painting had finally gone to a MYSTERY BUYER. 'See page 7 for an OPEN LETTER to MR JASPER JELLIT.'

'Oh snakes' elbows!' said Jasper, but he turned to page seven.

'MR JELLIT, YOU SHOULD BE ASHAMED OF YOURSELF!' thundered the letter. 'On behalf of the people of Woodford WE MUST TELL YOU that people should not keep DANGEROUS DOGS if they CAN NOT or WILL NOT keep them UNDER CONTROL.'

'Snakes' elbows and armpits,' said Jasper, who didn't care if he annoyed people. He was beginning to feel hungry now and was sorry he had sent his breakfast away. He turned again to the front of the paper and carefully studied the picture of the Mystery Buyer with his flattened-down hair and his dark glasses. It had been taken at the very end of the auction and the man was bellowing into his mobile phone. There was a small black and white cat perched on his head.

'I'm sure I've seen that cat somewhere before,' Jasper said to himself. 'I don't know where, but it looks familiar.'

Suddenly a light bulb went off in Jasper's head, as he realised that if he knew who owned the cat, then he would know who had bought the Haverford-Snuffley Angel.

And if he knew that...

DANDELION IN THE GARDEN

While Jasper, Wilf and Mrs Haverford-Snuffley were recovering from the auction, Dandelion spent a pleasant morning all alone in the garden of Barney's house. For a while she lay asleep with the hot sun warming her fur. When she awoke she chased some birds but in a half-hearted fashion because she was not a very good hunter. All the birds that came to Barney's garden knew this and they teased her, the robin and the chaffinch and the blackbird. They let her stalk them as though she were a tiger or a leopard but then when she was within a whisker of pouncing, they would fly away up into the branches of the great copper beech tree.

When she became tired of this, Dandelion settled down near the gates of the back garden and started to wash herself. If you had seen her there that morning you would have thought what a tidy-looking cat she was. Dandelion was black with a white bib and socks and a white splodge over her nose. The strange thing is that there are thousands and thousands of cats that fit this description, and yet they are all different. Certainly Barney would have been able to pick Dandelion out of a field full of black cats with white bibs and socks and splodges, because he knew her and loved her. She washed herself with her eyes closed, licking her paw and wiping it over her face, paying special attention to her ears. But when she opened her eyes again, Dandelion got the shock of her life!

There, on the other side of the gate, so near to her, were the two big dogs who had been at the auction. All at once they started barking madly. Leaping to her feet, Dandelion arched her back and spat and hissed. She looked angry but she was really terrified. All around Barney's garden was a high stone wall and in a single bound, *hop*! Dandelion was on top of it, staring down at the two dogs. They were still barking at the tops of their voices and she hissed at them again, but she felt safe now that she knew they couldn't reach her. As she sat gazing down coldly something very odd indeed happened.

A thought formed in her mind, but it wasn't Dandelion's thought.

'Please don't be angry.'

'How strange!'

Immediately she could see the difference between them, between the 'How strange!' which was definitely her own, and the 'Please don't be angry,' which most certainly wasn't.

'We don't want to hurt you.' This wasn't hers either. The two dogs had stopped barking now and were sitting staring up at her with soft, pleading eyes. How extraordinary! Could it really be possible…?

Dandelion decided to try a little experiment. 'Hello, my name is Dandelion,' she thought, feeling foolish as she did so, because of course she knew her own name. All of a sudden, two more thoughts popped into her head.

'Hello Dandelion.'

'What a beautiful name.'

Goodness – it was possible! The dogs started barking again but she realised now that they were excited rather than angry. Dandelion was very excited too. 'Thank you,' she thought. 'What are your names?'

'I'm Cannibal and this is Bruiser.'

'Hello Cannibal. Hello Bruiser.' The cat made a huge effort not to think about what terrible names these were because she didn't want to hurt their feelings, so instead she thought, 'I saw you both at the auction yesterday.'

With that her head was full of delighted laughter, so much of it, flooding out everything else like a great river breaking its banks.

'Oooh, that was good fun!' came the thought at last as the merriment ebbed away.

'The look on his face when you smashed his paddle!'

'Serves him right!'

'It isn't his real name, you know.'

'What is it then?' thought Dandelion.

'Jimmy. Jimmy Jellit. He thinks it isn't posh enough so he calls himself Jasper.'

'Wish I could change my name. I'm not really a Bruiser.'

'And I'm not a Cannibal.'

'If it comes to that, I'm not a Dandelion,' thought the cat to comfort them and again her head was filled with laughter.

'If you had the choice, what would you like to be called?'

'I see myself as a Rex rather than a Cannibal.'

But the other dog stared at the ground and it was some moments before a small faint thought finally drifted into Dandelion's mind. 'I know this must sound foolish but I'd like to be called...I think my name was always supposed to be...Snuggles.'

'Gosh! You don't look too snuggly!' The thought was out before Dandelion could stop herself.

'I could try,' thought Bruiser, lifting her head and staring with her gentle brown eyes at the cat. 'If someone loved me and snuggled me and cuddled me, I'm sure I'd become one of the snuggliest dogs in the whole world.'

'Will you be my friends?' thought Dandelion.

With that the dogs jumped up and started to bark loudly. 'Oh yes please! We would love that!'

Dandelion was delighted too. Although she was extremely happy living with Barney and Wilf, sometimes it was a bit lonely, because Barney was so shy and no one ever came to the house. 'Will you come and visit me?'

'We'll try. Jasper doesn't let us out much on our own. We were only able to sneak away this morning because he's in bed in a great big huff.'

'Oh I'm so happy that you're going to be our friend!'

At that very moment the back door of the house opened and Barney came out. He had heard the dogs barking and there they were, jumping up and down outside the gates, with Dandelion sitting on the wall high above them.

'Bad dogs! Shoo! Shoo! Go home!' By standing on his tiptoes, Barney could just about reach the cat, and he scooped her up.

'No, leave me, please! I want to stay here, I'm with my friends,' she thought. But it didn't work with humans, only with other animals. As she wriggled and mewed in Barney's arms he didn't understand what the matter was; he thought she was afraid.

'There there, poor little Dandelion cat,' and he turned again to Cannibal and Bruiser who had stuck their snouts through the railings of the gate. 'Bad dogs!' he said again. 'Go home! Shoo!'

They watched as he walked up the garden path holding Dandelion and thought how nice it must be to have an owner who cared for you like that, even if he didn't always understand what you wanted. They waited until the back door of the house was closed and then sat there looking at it for some moments before finally drifting away.

BOOM!

On Sunday afternoon Jasper went creeping around Woodford looking for the black and white cat that had been sitting on the Mystery Buyer's head. Almost immediately he found it. To his astonishment it was sitting in the front window of his old teacher Mr Kelly's house. Good Gobstoppers! Was it possible that he was the Haverford-Snuffley Angel's new owner? Old Jelly-Belly-Kelly? He sneaked up to the window to have a closer look at the cat. Yes, there was no doubt about it: it was black with a white bib and socks and a splodge over its nose. This was definitely the cat he had seen at the auction!

Just at that moment, he heard someone coming out of the front door of the house. His old teacher had never quite forgiven Jasper for putting a toad in his desk and mice in his coat pockets and for a thousand other mean tricks. To this day old Jelly-Belly used to chase Jasper down the street when he saw him, waving a cane and shouting, 'Hi you boy! Come here!' And so as soon as he heard the door opening, Jasper nipped smartly around the corner of the house and ran off up the road.

He stopped to get his breath back outside the chocolate shop. But no! It was impossible! There, sitting on the step, was ANOTHER cat and it was also black with a white bib and socks and a splodge over its nose! It looked exactly like both the cat at the auction and the cat in Mr Kelly's house. Jasper picked it up to have a closer look. One of its socks was longer than the other one. Did the auction cat have two socks the same length? Jasper couldn't remember. Its bib went the whole way down to its tummy. Perhaps the other cat had a shorter bib? Jasper wasn't sure. He was eyeball to eyeball with the cat now, who stared coldly at him.

'Has an angel come to live in your house?' Jasper whispered.

In reply the cat lashed out, dragged its claws down his cheek.

'Ow! That hurt, you little monster!' He let the

creature fall to the ground and it slunk off.

As Jasper turned away a third cat darted across the road and jumped up on to a wall. It was also black with a white bib and socks and a splodge over its nose and as soon as he saw it he burst into tears. This cat on the wall really was Dandelion but there was no way Jasper could know this. They all looked so alike, he thought; there was absolutely no way of telling them apart. He wondered if they were doing it deliberately. Jasper had never liked cats. Dragging his feet with misery, he gave up and went home.

There were no coins or bank notes or gold in Jasper's dreams that night, only cats: thousands and thousands of black and white cats. Each one was different from the others in only the smallest detail and it was impossible for him to know which was the one cat he needed to find. They swirled through Jasper's mind, chasing their tails or washing themselves, snoozing or purring. Suddenly one of them spoke directly to him.

'Do you really want to know which one of us you saw at the auction? Well then, we shall tell you.' With one voice, every last cat of all the

thousands and thousands shouted, 'IT WAS ME!'
Helpless with laughter, they fell around the place,
and with a loud scream, Jasper woke up.

Because he had slept so badly he was still tired
on the Monday morning, and even more grumpy
than usual. To make matters worse he had to go
to work that day. As his car moved through the
forest towards the factory he was once more in a
deep sulk.

Mr Smith greeted Jasper at the door of
his office. 'Let's get straight down to business,
shall we?'

Together they went through an order form.

'Hand guns, how many of those do you want?'

'Dunno.'

'I can let you have four hundred.'

'All right.'

'And what about stun guns, the same number?'

'I suppose so.' Jasper wasn't really paying
attention as he sat there with his lower lip stuck
out. Eventually Mr Smith put his pen down.

'Couldn't believe what happened at that
auction the other day,' he said. 'I mean, *Mystery
Buyer*, my granny. Everyone knows it has to be
that piano man.'

Jasper almost fell off his chair. 'Barney Barrington?'

'Yes, him,' said Mr Smith, staring hard at Jasper. 'He's got a black and white cat. He sent that little fat fellow that works for him to do the business. Wilf Somethingorother. Criminal type. Violent, from what it says in the papers. Ooh yes, a nasty piece of work, he is,' and Mr Smith shuddered at the thought. 'And above all, Barney Barrington's the only person in Woodford who's got enough money to buy himself a stupid little thing like that, just because it takes his fancy. Apart from yourself, of course.' And he smiled at Jasper, briefly showing his gold tooth. 'You'd have to be thick not to work it out. I mean it's obvious, isn't it?'

'Obvious,' said Jasper, who had gone very pale.

'It should have been yours,' Mr Smith said softly. 'You was robbed, Jasper. Robbed.' They sat in silence for a few moments and then Mr Smith picked up his pen again. 'Anyway, where were we? Machine guns.'

They continued to fill in the order form but Jasper found it impossible to concentrate. After some time Mr Smith put his pen down again.

'Silly me,' he said. 'Here I am nattering on about boring old assault rifles and hand grenades and forgetting to show you our newest and most exciting product.' From the drawer of his desk he took a bright red object the size of a pea. He held it out so that Jasper could inspect it, and then he stood up. The two men crossed to the door of the room.

Like all the doors in the factory it was stout and strong with a heavy lock. Mr Smith turned the key and then invited Jasper to try the handle, like a magician asking a member of the audience to make quite sure that the top hat was empty before he went on to produce a rabbit from it. The door was tightly locked.

'Now watch this carefully.' Mr Smith removed the key and pushed the red object into the keyhole. 'Stand well back please. Five, four, three, two, one...'

BOOM! In the air between Mr Smith and Jasper the word appeared in large red letters. The door flew open wide – and as all of this happened, there was complete silence in the room. The word looked as though it were made of coloured light. It hovered there for a moment and then slowly started to fade and dissolve, like the moment when a firework dies against a black sky. 'Good, isn't it? We've discovered the way to turn things you can hear into things you can see.'

At Jasper's feet was a little pile of red dust. He was too astonished to say anything. Mr Smith put his face up close and spoke softly, urgently.

'Take it!' he said. 'If somebody has something you want and you can't have it, just take it! There's no other way.' His voice was hoarse now and even Jasper found it frightening to have Mr Smith's cold face so close to his. 'Even if you have to use force it doesn't matter. If you want something Jasper, there's only one way to get it:

'Just take it!'

PICNIC

The following day was hot with a clear blue sky and for once Barney didn't feel like playing his piano after breakfast. Instead he threw the window of his bedroom open wide and looked out into the garden where Wilf was working. There was a pleasant grassy smell because he was cutting the lawn. Dandelion was also there, sunning herself and chasing birds. Afterwards when Wilf moved on to the flowerbeds, he stopped from time to time to talk to people who were passing the house.

A couple wheeling their new baby in a pram paused so that Wilf could admire her. A short while later the postman came by with his huge leather satchel. Some little children stopped and gave Wilf a boiled sweet out of a paper bag. In return he picked Dandelion up and held her so that they could stroke her head and tickle her tummy. Even from where he was, high up above the garden, Barney could hear the cat purring with delight. An extremely old lady came past and Wilf gave her a huge yellow rose.

When he brought the lunch up later he would tell Barney all the news he had heard from the passers-by, all the strange and funny things that were happening in Woodford. It was the same when Wilf went shopping, for he didn't just bring home loaves and potatoes and apples and eggs. He brought tales of how a long bright snake had been found in a box of pineapples at the greengrocers and how everyone had run out into the street screaming. Without Wilf, Barney would never have known that the baker's granny was having her hundredth birthday, nor about her birthday cake and how huge it had to be to hold all the candles. No one else would have told him about the single pink flamingo that appeared in the public park of Woodford one day, and disappeared the next. It was never seen in the town again and people would have thought they had imagined it, had it not been for the few pink feathers left behind.

Barney turned away from the window and looked at his room. There was his great piano, black and silent. The Haverford-Snuffley Angel hung nearby. There was the miniature tree, there were his many books. Barney loved these things and he realised how lucky he was to have them, together with all his other paintings and his beautiful house. But today he realised that it wasn't enough. Barney was lonely.

At lunch time Wilf appeared wheeling the trolley. On the top level were two mushroom pizzas, on the bottom was a grilled mackerel for the cat. Whistling a little tune, he set the table and they all three settled down to eat, because they always had their meals together now.

'I saw you talking to all the passers-by. What did they say to you?' Barney asked.

'The postman told me that someone wrote an address on a banana the other day, stuck a stamp on it and posted it. The new baby's only five days old and she's going to be called Minnie. The children are going on a school trip to the seaside next week. I gave a rose to the lady because she doesn't have a garden at her house and hasn't got enough money to buy herself flowers.

'And you,' Wilf said, cutting himself a big wedge of pizza. 'What news have you got for me?'

'Why nothing,' Barney said.

'It's a pity. There are lots of nice people in Woodford. It would be good if you made friends with some of them.'

'Oh I couldn't, I just couldn't.'

'Course you could,' Wilf said. 'What about that Philomena Phelan woman who works in the gallery. I bet she'd love to be your friend. She's a good person and you'd have lots to talk about because she likes paintings too.'

'I couldn't,' Barney said again, and he went red and looked at his hands.

Wilf simply couldn't understand how anyone could be so shy. He thought it was silly. 'You should get out more,' he said.

'I do go out. I go out on my bike.'

'But I bet you just whizz past people and never say hello, much less stop to talk to them. Am I right? Is that what he does, Pussens?'

Dandelion looked up from her mackerel and nodded her head.

Barney looked so sad that Wilf felt sorry for him. 'Tell you what,' he suggested. 'Because it's such a lovely day why don't we go for a picnic later, down by the river.'

'Thank you, Wilf! I should like that very much indeed.'

And so in the late afternoon they set off together, Barney carrying a rug for them to sit on and Wilf carrying the picnic hamper. Dandelion trotted ahead of them with her tail straight up in the air. They found a quiet spot near a bridge and settled themselves down on the sloping green bank of the river. Wilf unbuckled the hamper and opened it out. Inside there was a red and white checked tablecloth, white plates and napkins, glasses, knives and forks. There was a special plate for Dandelion, and a gammon steak. For Barney and Wilf there were sausage rolls and cheese sandwiches, oranges, crisps and a chocolate swiss roll. Wilf tied a string to the neck of their bottle of lemonade and floated it in the river so that it would stay cool.

'We should have invited some other people along,' he said. 'One of the good things about having a picnic with your friends is that everyone brings along food. Then you can share it out and there are always lots of lovely surprises.'

'If O-Haru came to a picnic she might bring some raw fish,' Barney said. 'It's her favourite food. But I don't think anybody else would want to share that.'

Dandelion was listening to this. 'I would like to share it,' she thought. 'If O-Haru were here she could have some of our chocolate swiss roll and I could have some of her raw fish.'

'She's ever so nice,' Barney went on, 'and so clever. She knows how to make animals out of folded paper, foxes and birds. It makes me sad to think that I'll never see her again. She lives so far away, right on the other side of the world.'

Just at that moment, Dandelion happened to glance up and was astonished by what she saw. For who was sitting on the bridge, gazing down at the little party? Only Cannibal and Bruiser!

'Hello Dandelion.'

'Why hello! I was thinking only just this minute how much nicer it would be to have friends along on a picnic, and here you are.'

'We'd love to join you,' came Cannibal's wistful thought. 'We'd bring our own food. We'd bring meat pies.'

'If you wanted, we could swap them with you for some of those sausage rolls. They look very tasty,' Bruiser added.

The poor dogs were always hungry because Jasper never gave them enough to eat.

'I wish I could give you a sausage roll each here and now,' she thought.

'Don't worry. We know we can't join in with your picnic. Your master doesn't like us,' Cannibal thought.

'Nobody likes us.'

'That isn't true. I like you!' Dandelion thought. 'I like you hugely.'

Barney had finished his cheese sandwiches and was eating a bag of crisps while Wilf tugged on the string of the lemonade bottle. Neither of them had noticed the dogs and the cat did her best not to draw attention to them. Cannibal and Bruiser themselves sat quietly and took care not to bark. 'But we didn't come today to have a picnic with you. We've come to warn you. Dandelion, you're in danger! You and everyone in your house!'

'This very night!'

'Beware, Dandelion! Beware!'

The poor creature was so shocked to hear this that she jumped up. All her fur was on end and her green eyes were open wide.

Immediately Barney saw that something was

wrong. 'What is it, my dear Puss?' he asked, and he followed the line of her gaze up to the bridge. 'Oh no, it's those nasty, wicked dogs again. Shoo, shoo! Bad dogs, go home. Help me, Wilf. Frighten them off.'

Thinking to protect her, Barney picked Dandelion up and dropped her head first down the front of his buttoned-up cardigan. 'Oh really, this man was silly sometimes, silly beyond belief,' the cat thought as she struggled to turn herself right-sides up again. 'He means well but he gets it wrong every time.' Her face now full of cardigan, now full of belly, she could hear Wilf chasing the dogs: 'Scram! Go on, hoppit!'

The dogs had started to bark as soon as Barney shouted at them, but they sounded fainter and farther away at every moment. By the time Dandelion's cross little whiskered face popped out again above the top button of Barney's cardigan the dogs were nowhere to be seen.

But still their terrible warning rang in her ears. 'Beware, Dandelion! Beware!'

A SHOCK IN THE NIGHT

At a quarter to ten that night, Dandelion hopped on to Barney's knee and stared up at him. Her clear green eyes were wide and anxious. He kissed her between the ears and stroked her under the chin.

'Oh my dear Dandelion,' he said. 'If I were granted three wishes, one of them would be that you could talk to me. Often I look at you and I feel as if you're trying so hard to tell me something, but I don't know what it is.'

The problem tonight was that Dandelion didn't know either. She knew that something was going to happen because the dogs had warned her, but she couldn't even begin to guess what it might be. Neither she nor Barney knew that as they sat together on the sofa something very strange indeed was taking place at the back door of the house. In the blackness of the night the word *BOOM!* suddenly and silently appeared in huge red letters, floating in the air beside the lock. The door flew open and the word crumbled away into coloured dust. Dressed all in black, Jasper Jellit slipped into the darkened house and started moving like a shadow from room to room.

Ding! The clock on Barney's mantelpiece chimed ten o'clock. 'Come along, Puss. Cocoa time.'

When they stepped out into the long corridor and Barney switched on the first light, the cat's heart was beating so hard she thought he must surely hear it. But he simply stopped as usual to admire the painting of the man in the dark red robe and velvet hat, before passing by and switching on the second light. He glanced at the picture of the bowl of wood strawberries but when he moved on to the salmon, the cat paid no heed even though it was her favourite painting. Feeling nervous, she turned and looked behind her, back down the corridor with the closed door of Barney's room at the far end.

As they moved on, all at once Dandelion felt the fur rise on the back of her neck. They weren't alone. There was someone else in the house tonight, she was sure of it, absolutely sure. She looked behind her again and got a tremendous shock, for there, standing in front of the painting of the young man, was Jasper!

She gave a loud wild mew and Barney jumped in surprise. 'Goodness me, cat! Did I stand on your foot? Did I hurt you?' She mewed again but Jasper had already disappeared through the door between the picture of the man and the picture of the wood strawberries and was hiding there.

'Come along, Dandelion.' They reached the end of the first corridor and went down the spiral staircase to the second level.

'I know Wilf has a point when he says I should have friends but I do so love my beautiful paintings,' said Barney as he plodded slowly along, admiring them and turning on the lights as he went.

Dandelion looked over her shoulder. There he was again! Jasper glared at the cat and put his finger to his lips, bidding her to be quiet. In response she mewed again, a long low horrible howl. Jasper stuck his tongue out at her, before darting into another doorway just as Barney turned around. 'My little Dandelion, what is it? I simply don't know what's got into you tonight.'

He picked the cat up and carried her in his arms for the rest of the way, with her head looking over his shoulder, so she could see Jasper as he followed them down to the kitchen, sneaking in and out of the rooms between where the paintings hung.

'Behind you!' Dandelion thought. If only this trick worked with human beings! If only she could plant an idea in Barney's mind as she could with Cannibal and Bruiser. 'BEHIND YOU!'

At last they arrived in the kitchen, the whole house now ablaze with light.

'Come in, my friends, come in!'

'Hello Wilf. I'm really worried about the cat tonight. She's behaving very strangely. I know she got a fright with the dogs down by the river but that was hours ago and she's still so fidgety and nervous. You see? She's not drinking her milk.' And although her suppertime saucer was there as usual, Dandelion was too upset to touch it.

'What's up with you Pussens, eh?' said Wilf as he prepared Barney's cocoa. 'If you like I'll take her along to the vet in the morning.'

The vet! Oh no! Dandelion hated going to the

vet. 'Look, you see how restless she is,' Barney said as she crossed to the kitchen door and went back out into the corridor.

The cheek of him! There was Jasper, walking up and down staring at all the paintings. When he saw that Dandelion was alone, he didn't hide. 'Push off, cat,' he hissed. 'Don't you know when you're not wanted?'

Suddenly Dandelion realised why he was there and what the dogs had wanted to tell her.

Jasper was going to steal the Haverford-Snuffley Angel.

He had wanted to buy it at the auction but hadn't been able to do so and now he was going to take it anyway. Stretching out his right leg he gave Dandelion a little kick. 'Go on pussycat, get lost.'

In reply to this she opened her mouth as wide as she possibly could. From where Jasper was standing she seemed to disappear, leaving only a wet pink mouth ringed with a ferocious set of pointed teeth. From this mouth came a truly horrible sound.

'MEEEEAAAUUUUGHHHHOOOOHHHUUU RRRRMAAARRRWAAARRROOOOOOUUU!' It was extraordinary to think that so small and sweet a cat could make so loud and dreadful a noise. Appalled, Jasper stuck his fingers in his ears. Dandelion caught her breath and did it again.

'WAAAAHHHHUUUOOOOMMAAAWOOOOO AAAAAAMARRROOOOOO!'

Barney shot out of the kitchen holding his mug of cocoa. 'Stop that this very minute, Dandelion! I never heard such a racket in my life. Why are you being so naughty tonight? Come now, follow me and behave yourself.'

Jasper, of course, had disappeared again. Barney couldn't carry both the cat and the cocoa and so Dandelion trotted at his heels, turning around from time to time to see if Jasper was still following them. Yes, there he was, sneaking from one room to the next behind them in the darkness as Barney switched off each of the lights in turn. Dandelion knew that the Haverford-Snuffley Angel was in Barney's room. She was in a foul temper now with Jasper because he had kicked her and she was determined not to let him get his hands on the painting. But how was she to stop him?

They reached the top floor of the house and

moved slowly down the corridor. At the far end they could see the shut door of the bedroom. 'I do hope you're going to settle down and sleep,' said Barney.

Suddenly Dandelion realised that, being a cat, she had one big advantage over the two men: she could see in the dark. She looked round just in time to see Jasper disappear into the room between the painting of the strawberries and the painting of the young man. Barney switched out the last light in the corridor. He had left on the lamps in the bedroom so that when he opened the door he would be able to see clearly again. But in that moment of total darkness, between his turning off the last light and opening the door, Dandelion knew that the moment had come to act!

She shot from his side and darted into the room where Jasper was hiding. It was pitch black but she could see that he was standing in the middle of the floor, quite lost, not knowing where any of the furniture was. She gave a sharp, savage mew and leapt at him, landing on his face.

'Arrgh! Uugh! I can't breathe!'

Dandelion wrapped her paws tightly around

his head and held on as if her life depended on it while Jasper spun round and round the room, not knowing where he was and completely unable to shake her off. Dandelion remembered watching children on the merry-go-round at Woodford Fair and how she had wondered what it must be like to go round and round and round like that. 'Now I know,' she thought as she saw the bookcase go past for the twentieth time, and she clung on to Jasper's head, as though it were the pole of a prancing wooden horse.

And then she lost her grip. She flew one way across the room while Jasper flew in the opposite direction. As she landed on the table and slid along it like a cowboy's drink in a Wild West bar she heard the window breaking. There was a long wild cry. Then *Crump!* Something hit the ground outside. Then *Crash!* Dandelion skidded into a vase at the end of the table and it fell to the floor in a million bits. But the cat kept going, and slid right off the end of the table and into a bookcase that toppled over just as Barney opened the door and switched on the light.

What a sight met his eyes! The bookcase was falling forward like a great tree being cut down in a forest, and book after book tumbled to the floor. The window was broken and the vase was smashed, and sitting there in the middle of all this mess and destruction was Dandelion.

'I saved your angel for you,' she thought, but she knew it was no use.

'You bad cat! You naughty creature! You bad, bad cat!'

FUDGE

'Been in the wars, eh Jasper?' said Mr Smith.

Jasper didn't reply but scowled across the desk.

'Those are nasty-looking scratches on your face. Lucky whatever did it didn't put your eye out. For how long is your arm going to be in that sling?'

'The doctor's taking the plaster off tomorrow,' Jasper said and Mr Smith smiled brightly

'You'll be back in business then, won't you? Ready for action. Ready for anything.'

On the desk was a glass dish filled with squares of fudge. Mr Smith picked one up, removed its cellophane wrapper and popped it in his mouth. Jasper moved to take one as well but Mr Smith shook his head and pulled the dish away with a mysterious smile. And then right before Jasper's very eyes, something quite remarkable happened. Mr Smith started to disappear. First the top of his head went, then his eyes, his nose, his smiling mouth with its gold tooth. Now headless, his neck melted away and then his chest.

'Good, isn't it?' said a voice from nowhere.

'It's incredible,' Jasper said. 'It's quite, quite incredible.'

Mr Smith now seemed to have completely vanished. Jasper imagined that the bottom half of him was still disappearing behind the desk when all of a sudden a voice shouted in his ear. 'BOO!'

Jasper jumped in fright and heard a little chuckle. Now that he was invisible, Mr Smith had sneaked around the desk to tease Jasper. It was incredible and it was horrible and it was wonderful all at the same time. Jasper thought of all the things he could do with the fudge, as a pair of black shoes appeared on the floor beside him. There were feet in the shoes and now legs in grey trousers. From the floor up Mr Smith once more became visible until there he was, standing before Jasper still smiling his mysterious smile.

'How much?' Jasper said immediately.

'Not cheap,' said Mr Smith.

'How much?' Jasper asked again.

Mr Smith named his price and Jasper said, 'Ow!' as though he had toothache. 'Is that for a whole box of fudge?'

Mr Smith shook his head sadly. 'That's for a single square. Told you it wasn't cheap.'

Jasper sat there thinking.

'It's very new stuff,' Mr Smith said. 'The boys in the backroom are still working on it. This is the weakest variety,' and he pointed to the fudge in the dish. 'I only use it for demonstration purposes. But even the effect of the strongest doesn't last for very long.'

'So if I wanted to be invisible for an hour or two I'd have to eat a lot of fudge to start with?'

'Exactly. And there's the danger that it might wear off at the wrong moment, that you'd start to become visible again when you didn't want to be. Could be embarrassing.'

'Couldn't you eat some more then? Top up the effect?'

'I suppose so,' said Mr Smith.

'Does it work with animals?'

'It works wonderfully well with animals. We gave some to the factory cat and it disappeared for a whole day. The poor mice had a terrible time with an invisible cat running around the place. But the boys are still working on it,' Mr Smith said again. 'The product isn't ready yet. I think you should wait.'

'No,' said Jasper.

Because Jasper couldn't wait for anything. Often when he woke in the middle of the night, he rang for the maid to bring him his breakfast because he couldn't wait until the morning. He had once even celebrated Christmas in the middle of summer, with a tree and a turkey and presents, simply because he couldn't bear to wait until December. 'I want the fudge and I want it now.'

'Suit yourself,' said Mr Smith. 'You'll be needing at least four boxes,' and he did a little sum on a notepad that was sitting on the desk, then told Jasper the final mind-boggling price.

'I'll take an extra box,' Jasper said just to remind Mr Smith how rich he was. Mr Smith was impressed.

'It is a remarkable product,' he said as Jasper got his wallet out, 'and you're a remarkable man. You see it's all very well to become invisible; it's knowing what to do then, that's the test. It's having the imagination. It's thinking big.'

'I know exactly what I'm going to do.'

'I bet you do,' said Mr Smith, buttering up Jasper. 'I bet you do. What are you planning?'

The boxes of fudge were on the table now and Jasper started to pack them into his briefcase. He smiled at Mr Smith and gave a slow wink. 'That,' he said, 'would be telling.'

STRANGE EVENTS AT
BARNEY'S HOUSE

The morning after Jasper's attempt to steal the Haverford-Snuffley Angel, Wilf fixed the broken window and put the books back on the shelves. There was nothing to be done about the vase except to throw the pieces in the bin. Dandelion was put in her basket and taken to see the vet, a stern woman who plucked the cat up by the scruff of its neck. They stared at each other, eyeball to eyeball, as Wilf explained what had happened the night before.

'What do you feed it?'

'She eats very well,' said Wilf. 'On a typical day she might have grilled pork sausages for her breakfast, then baked haddock for lunch with a dish of fresh cream as a mid-afternoon snack.'

'What?' cried the vet. She let go of Dandelion's

neck and the cat dropped like a stone back into the basket. 'Baked haddock, your granny! No wonder this cat is nervous and difficult. It eats far too much rich food. From now on give it only a saucer of milk in the morning, one small simple meal for its lunch, and milk again at night. It also has to take two of these yellow pills three times a day. I know they're rather big and it'll hate having to swallow them but take no nonsense from it.'

Dandelion couldn't believe her ears and began to wail with misery.

'You see?' said the vet. 'Spoilt. Spoilt rotten. It'll do you good, Miss Puss, to know a little hardship.' (People tend to like either dogs or cats. The vet liked dogs.)

She hadn't finished either. From a drawer in her desk she took a small red leather harness. 'It's got a nasty slouch too,' she said. 'Make it wear this at all times.'

'How will that help?' asked Wilf in surprise.

'It just will,' said the vet. A short brutal struggle followed as she put the harness on Dandelion. Wilf thought it was quite normal for a cat to slouch. There was nothing he hated more than having to wear a shirt and tie so he could imagine how Dandelion felt, and was extremely sorry for her.

In the days that followed, life returned to normal in Barney's house and another week rolled by. Monday came and the sun rose hot and bright over Woodford. Just after dawn a large white van drove into the road beside Barney's house and came to a halt. This would have been a most unremarkable event and not worth mentioning were it not for one significant detail. The van was empty. It was driven down the road but there was no one at the steering wheel. Stranger still, once it was parked the doors opened and closed but no one got out.

The milkman had already done his rounds. At about eight o'clock Wilf opened the front door to bring in the bottles from the step. As he bent down, his hands brushed against something warm and hairy close to the ground. He heard a panting sound and could smell expensive *eau de cologne*. But there was nothing and no one there. The front step was completely empty except for the usual two white bottles. Goose-pimples rose on Wilf's arms. He picked up the milk but as he turned to go back inside, someone or something bumped against him, pushed him rudely aside and swept into the hall. Wilf could feel all of this but still there was nothing to be seen. 'Oo-er!' His hair stood straight up on end in fright. 'What on earth was that?!'

'This is a very old house,' he said to Barney as he served breakfast a short time later. 'When you bought it, did they say anything to you about ghosts?'

Barney looked up in surprise from his cinnamon toast. 'Of course not. Everybody knows there's no such thing as a ghost.'

'There might be,' argued Wilf.

'Well there isn't. Not in this house anyway. Why do you ask?'

Wilf thought about what had happened on the step. He must have imagined it. 'I was just wondering,' he said.

After breakfast, Wilf went back to the kitchen and Barney settled down to play the piano. Dandelion sat beside him listening. From time to time her tummy rumbled so loudly it could be heard over the music. Poor Dandelion was tremendously hungry. It would be hours until lunch time, she reflected, staring miserably at the clock, and even then all she would get was a couple of spoonfuls of horrible tinned cat food.

With that, a thought came into her mind.

'Dandelion! Dandelion! It's us – Cannibal and Bruiser.' It was loud and clear, but the dogs were nowhere to be seen.

'Where are you?' she thought. 'Are you down in the garden?'

'No, we're here in the room, right beside you. We're invisible. I know it's hard to believe but it's true.' And with that, the cat felt a huge rough paw pat her gently on the head.

'How can this be?'

'Jasper gave us sweets to eat and we disappeared. He's in the house right this minute and he's invisible too. He's going to steal all the paintings – everything, not just the Haverford-Snuffley Angel. He's got a big white van parked outside to take them away.'

'This is terrible news! What shall we do? Oh what shall we do?' thought Dandelion.

'Jasper brought us along because he's afraid of you,' thought Bruiser. 'And he thinks you'll be afraid of us.'

'That's right,' added Cannibal. 'He said, "You

deal with the cat and leave the people to me." But don't worry, we're on your side, Dandelion. We'll do all we can to help you.'

'You should try to warn your owner,' thought Bruiser.

'It won't be easy,' thought the cat, remembering the last time she had tried to let Barney know Jasper was in the house and up to no good. She looked to where he was still contentedly playing his piano.

'Do what you can,' thought Bruiser. 'We'd best go and see where Jasper is. We'll catch up with you later.' Again Dandelion felt a rough, comforting paw touch her on the head. The door of the room, which was ajar, opened wider as the two invisible dogs slipped out on to the landing.

Dandelion hopped up on to the piano and sat down at the end of the keyboard, staring hard at Barney. She was wearing her red leather harness, which was tight and uncomfortable. 'What is it, my dear? What do you want?' he said and he stopped playing, leaned over to tickle her chin. 'Why, how could I have forgotten? Your pills!'

Oh no! He crossed to the bedside table, picked up a brown glass jar and took from it two enormous yellow pills. 'Come along, Dandelion. Be a good cat and take your medicine.'

'You'll have to catch me first,' thought Dandelion, and with one bound she was at the top of the curtains. She hung there by her claws, mewing, while Barney tried to coax her down.

Meanwhile, down in the kitchen, Wilf was already preparing lunch. He had rolled out the pastry for an apple pie and was peeling and chopping the fruit when the kitchen door swung open. 'Must be a draught,' Wilf thought as he went over and pushed it closed again. Just at that moment he caught again the smell of *eau de cologne* he'd noticed when he was bringing in the milk. Had the ghost come back? he wondered.

As if in reply, the rolling pin rose off the table and floated in mid air. 'Eek! Help!' he cried as it moved towards him and then *Thwack!* Wilf's own rolling pin hit him hard on the head! He saw red lights and swirling stars, reeled backwards and almost fell over. The rolling pin was still hovering over his head. He saw it draw back to thump him again and with that Wilf started to run. Round and round the table he went with the rolling pin following him. Never in his life had he been so frightened. To be chased by a man with a rolling pin would be awful he thought, but somehow to be chased by the rolling pin itself was even worse.

Suddenly he noticed the door into the pantry and he threw himself on it. The door fell open and he tumbled straight into the small dark room, head first into a lemon jelly that had been left there to set. The rolling pin – it could be no one or nothing else – slammed the door shut and Wilf heard the key being turned in the lock. It was almost a relief to be sitting there on the floor in the darkness, with a fancy jelly mould on his head and lemon jelly slithering down the back of his neck. At least here he was safe.

Up in the bedroom, Barney had managed to catch Dandelion and to force one of the yellow pills into her. It was achieved with much wiggling and mewing and scratching on Dandelion's part, and much coaxing and scolding and scrambling on Barney's. He was quite exhausted with the effort.

'I shall have to fetch Wilf to help me give you the second one, or it'll take all morning.'

Barney left the room with Dandelion at his heels to go to the kitchen. He was amazed to see that all the paintings had been removed from the wall and were stacked up neatly at the end of the passageway. Why on earth had Wilf done this? He hadn't asked him to, and Wilf hadn't mentioned anything about it. Puzzled, Barney continued along the corridor and went down the stairs. What a sight met his eyes on the second floor!

A picture in a heavy gold frame of a storm at sea was getting down from the wall all by itself. Several other paintings were already stacked up nearby. Barney watched open-mouthed and goggle-eyed as the seascape slid itself up the wall and then tilted out at the bottom. Slowly and gently it moved off and hovered in mid-air for a moment before lowering itself to the ground. It rested there as if it were tired and Barney noticed a curious and pleasant smell, a cross between pinecones and lemons. 'It's like a very good *eau de cologne*,' he said to himself. Suddenly the painting rose up again and floated along the corridor until it came to the stack of pictures, to which it carefully added itself.

'I'm dreaming,' Barney thought. 'I'm in my bed fast asleep and dreaming, with Dandelion curled up at the back of my knees. Any minute now the alarm clock will go off and Wilf will come into the room with tea and toast and muffins and marmalade and another ordinary day will begin.' But he knew in his heart that he wasn't dreaming and that this extraordinary day was completely real.

With that, out of nowhere, a pair of shoes appeared. It was an expensive-looking pair of men's shoes, in shiny black leather, and they were walking down the corridor from the stack of paintings to where Barney and Dandelion stood. The turn-ups on the bottom of a pair of trousers now appeared above the shoes. Barney gave a little squawk of fright, and the shoes came to a halt. Trousers were visible now, up as far as the knee.

'Snakes' elbows!' said a voice. There was a pause, followed by a rustling of sweet papers and then a chomping, guzzling noise. Immediately the trousers began to fade away from the knees down. Now there was only a pair of shoes and they started to walk again, once more heading straight for Barney.

Throughout all of this, Dandelion watched helplessly. She knew exactly what was happening, but there was nothing she could do to tell Barney or to stop it. 'Where are you?' she thought anxiously. 'Where are you, dogs?'

Just at that moment, she heard a panting sound and an answering thought popped into her mind.

'Sorry we're late,' gasped Cannibal. 'We were down in the kitchen trying to help Wilf but he's trapped in the pantry and we couldn't manage to unlock the door.'

'This isn't going well,' added Bruiser. 'Jasper's working much faster than we expected and I don't know how we're going to stop him.'

By now the shoes had disappeared again. Barney could hear the panting noise too and he felt something brush against his legs. A ghost! Wilf had asked him that very morning if there was a ghost in the house. He must have come across it too, but he hadn't said anything so as not to frighten Barney. But it was no use because Barney WAS frightened. Never before in all of his long life had he been so scared. 'Help!' he cried as another painting started to rise off the wall. 'HELP!!!' He scooped Dandelion up in his arms and raced away down the corridor to the stairs, back up to the top floor faster than she'd ever have believed possible.

'Oh this is useless,' the cat thought to herself in dismay as they crashed into the bedroom. Barney slammed the door closed and turned the key in the lock. 'I won't be able to do anything now to help Cannibal and Bruiser.' Jumping from his arms she scratched at the door and mewed and wailed.

'Don't cry, my little Dandelion, we're safe now,' Barney said. 'The ghost can't get at us here. But what about poor Wilf? And what about the paintings? Oh what a dreadful, dreadful morning this is turning out to be!'

IN THE POLICE STATION

The policeman and policewoman looked at each other. They looked at the black cat with a white bib and socks and a white splodge over its nose that was sitting on the counter of the police station. They looked at the two men on the other side of the counter. One was small and fat, with shiny dark eyes like black buttons and wild hair standing on end. The other was an elderly man with wispy grey hair, and his eyes were red because he had been crying.

'Let's go through all of this again, shall we,' said the policewoman, turning to the big leather-bound book in which she had just finished writing down the whole story. 'All your paintings have been stolen.'

'Yes,' said Barney tearfully.

'By a ghost.'

'Yes.'

'And this ghost was completely invisible,' said the policeman.

'Except for when it was a pair of shoes,' replied Barney.

'And a rolling pin,' added Wilf.

'And the, um, rolling pin threw a raspberry jelly at you,' said the policeman, pointing at Wilf with his pencil.

'It was a lemon jelly and it wasn't thrown at me. I fell into it when the rolling pin chased me into the pantry and locked the door.'

The policeman and woman looked at each other again. 'The rolling pin chased you into the pantry and locked the door,' the woman repeated.

'Yes.'

'Course it did,' said the policeman. 'Happens every day of the week.'

'Twice on Sundays,' said the policewoman. She bit her lip, clearly trying hard not to laugh, and looked down at the book again. 'And the rolling pin also chased you into the bedroom and locked you in there?' she said to Barney.

'No, that was the shoes. Only they were invisible again by then and they didn't really chase me, it was more that I ran away because I was frightened. I locked myself in the bedroom with the cat.'

'And you stayed there for almost the whole day,' said the policewoman, 'and when you came out you found that all your paintings had gone, every last one of them.'

'Yes,' said Barney, and he started to cry again.

'So you went downstairs and you found him,' she said, pointing at Wilf, 'locked in the pantry.'

'Yes.'

'With a jelly on his head.'

'Yes.'

'A lemon jelly.'

'Yes.'

'He having been chased there by a rolling pin.'

'Yes.'

Dandelion was wondering if the police were always as slow-witted as this when suddenly the policeman turned to her. 'And what about you, eh, Miss P. Cat?' and he jabbed her hard in the bib with a stubby finger. 'Maybe I should take a statement from you. What have you got to say for yourself?'

Dandelion drew herself up proudly and stared at him hard with her cold green eyes. She would have given eight of her nine lives there on the spot for the gift of speech. She imagined herself telling the police in a low calm voice exactly what had happened. 'It wasn't a ghost. It was Jasper Jellit. If you go over to his house you'll find all the paintings hidden there. He stole them. His dogs will back up my story.'

'We're waiting, Puss,' said the policeman, and he jabbed at her again, chuckling at his own wit in pretending to expect a cat to be of any help.

'*Eau de cologne,*' said the policewoman turning to Barney and Wilf. 'You both smelt *eau de cologne.*'

'We did, yes.'

'Smelt nice then, these shoes?' said the policeman and he tittered.

'What about the rolling pin?' giggled the policewoman. 'Suppose you'll be telling us next all rolling pins spray themselves behind the ears with *eau de cologne* every morning.'

'Course they do,' guffawed the policeman. 'Haven't you noticed that every time you go to the chemists you can't get anywhere near the perfume counter because of all the…all the…'

But he was laughing so much now that he

couldn't get the words out and the policewoman had to finish his sentence for him. 'Rolling pins!' she shrieked. 'Because of all the rolling pins!'

'*Parfum pour Homme. Pour Femme. Pour Rolling Pin!*'

'Ooh this is hilarious,' said the policewoman, wiping her eyes.

'Tell you what,' said the policeman to Barney, still helpless with laughter. 'When I find this invisible ghost, I'll put my hand on his shoulder and arrest him for you.'

'If you can find his shoulder,' gasped the policewoman. 'And I'll put it in handcuffs.'

'Ghosts don't have hands,' roared the policeman.

'Neither do...rolling pins,' screamed the policewoman, and they were off again, laughing until they wept.

'Oh deary me,' cried the policeman eventually, still gasping and giggling. 'Never in all my born days, never in all my many long years in the force have I heard such a complete and utter load of codswallop. I'd charge you pair with wasting police time,' he added, trying to look stern, 'were it not for the fact that I don't remember when I last had such a good laugh.'

'Now hoppit,' said the policewoman, 'and take the pussycat with you. Don't let me see you back in here again.'

'Course if the ghost comes in, we won't see it either,' said the policeman, 'because it's invisible.'

'Nor the shoes!'

'Nor the rolling pin!'

And as Barney, Wilf and Dandelion trudged home sadly, they could hear the laughter of the policeman and woman still floating up the street behind them.

THE BEST OF FRIENDS

Dandelion had sometimes thought that Barney's house was a bit lonely, because it was so big and no one ever came to visit. But after all the paintings had been stolen there were no two ways about it: it was a tremendously sad and gloomy place. Barney was completely heartbroken. The house was silent at all hours now because he was too upset even to play his piano. The long corridors where the paintings had hung were desolate and empty. Wilf was nervous all the time, terrified that the ghost would come back and chase him again. He was always looking over his shoulder now and the slightest sudden noise or unexpected movement made him jump in fright. Dandelion wandered alone wistfully from room to room. She still had to take the yellow pills and wear the hated red harness; was hungry all the time because she was given so little to eat.

Everything was miserable now, she thought.

Jasper, on the other hand, had never been happier. The day after the robbery he called the butler to his room. 'I'm going to throw a party,' he said. 'I've got something to celebrate.'

'Indeed Sir? And what might that be?' asked the butler politely.

'Not telling!' said Jasper. 'Wouldn't you like to know?' and he stuck out his tongue.

The butler gave a thin smile. 'I can't take much more of this,' he thought. 'Any day now, I'm going to climb over that wall in the middle of the night and run away.'

'It's going to have an Italian theme this time,' Jasper went on. 'Venice!' he cried.

As usual, no expense was spared. A vast network of canals was dug throughout Jasper's estate. They were flooded with water and a fleet of gondolas was brought in especially from Italy so that the guests could amuse themselves sailing up and down in the shiny black boats. The Prince of Venice was called a Doge and so of course Jasper had to be him. He ordered a suit of gold to wear, with which he was delighted, not realising it made him look like a total prat. A magnificent painted wooden barge to be rowed by fifty oarsmen was also bought so that he could make a spectacular entrance. The Doge had lived in a palace in Venice made of pink and white stone arranged in pretty patterns. Not to be outdone, Jasper made the whole of the front of his house look exactly the same by covering it with squares of pink and white marshmallow. The long-suffering dogs were kitted out in velvet robes, dark red for Cannibal and bottle green for Bruiser. Teams of Italian chefs sweated and toiled, turning out vast tangled heaps of spaghetti, made fragrant with fresh basil, and pizzas as big as cartwheels. The pastry cooks created extraordinary puddings made of sweetened cream cheese and candied fruit, the like of which had never before been seen in Woodford.

Late that night, Dandelion saw the firework display that brought the party to a close. After Barney had gone to sleep, she stood on the windowsill of the darkened bedroom with her front paws pressed against the pane and watched the spectacular explosions of coloured light unfold and fade against the night sky.

The following morning there was a special colour supplement in the *Woodford Trumpet,* full of photographs of the party. Barney leafed through it listlessly as he ate his bacon and eggs. Nothing interested him these days.

'Cheer up,' Wilf said. 'At least you've still got your angel,' and he nodded towards the bedside table. Because Barney had kept the new painting in his room it hadn't been stolen when Jasper took all the other pictures.

'I suppose you're right,' Barney said, and he stared at the Haverford-Snuffley Angel, with its bright eyes and vivid wings. 'But even so Wilf, even so…'

After drinking every single drop of the small saucer of milk that was all she now received, but before anyone had time to even think about the yellow pills, Dandelion slipped out of the house. 'I'll go and visit Cannibal and Bruiser,' she decided. 'Perhaps there'll be some food left over from the party.'

As soon as they saw her, the dogs knew what was in her mind. 'I'm sorry to disappoint you but there's not a sausage left,' Cannibal thought. 'The greedy guests scoffed the lot.'

'They even ate all the pink and white marshmallows off the front of the house,' added Bruiser.

'Never mind,' thought Dandelion, even as her tummy rumbled. 'It's nice just to be here with you.'

The cat and the dogs settled down under a tree together, to watch the army of workmen who were busy setting the garden to rights again. Already the shiny black gondolas were stacked up on a lorry to be taken away and the water had been drained from the canals. Soon the men would fill the empty trenches with soil and cover them with grass. Then the garden would look immaculate again, until the next time Jasper decided to throw one of his crazy parties.

Crack! All at once something flew past Dandelion's head, missing her literally by a whisker. What was it? *Crack!* It happened again, this time almost hitting her ear. They looked towards the house and saw to their horror that Jasper was leaning out of his bedroom and pointing a gun straight at them. *Crack!* He was shooting at Dandelion! Terrified, she took off and raced zigzagging across the lawns, desperate to get away. 'Attaboy, Cannibal!' Jasper shouted as the two dogs ran after the cat. 'Kill, Bruiser, kill!'

Panting and shocked, all the animals arrived at the high wall that enclosed Jasper's land. In a single bound Dandelion leapt to the top of it, and sat there trembling with fear.

'We're sorry about this,' the dogs thought, 'so very sorry.'

'I know it's not your fault,' Dandelion replied, 'but I hope you'll understand if I don't come to visit you again. Will you come and visit me instead?'

'But your owner doesn't like us,' thought Bruiser.

'Yes, but the worst he'll do is to shoo you away,' the cat argued. 'Barney would never try to shoot you. Oh please come, I'll be so lonely if you don't.'

'We'll visit you, Dandelion,' the two dogs promised. 'We won't let you down.'

They kept their word the very next day, and Barney noticed them just as Wilf was wheeling in the trolley for lunch. 'Those horrible dogs are back, they're pestering the cat again.'

But when he moved to the window so that he could shout at them and scare them off Wilf said, 'No, wait a minute. Look.' Because something quite remarkable was taking place. Far from frightening or annoying the cat, they were all three quite happily playing together.

'Well I never!' exclaimed Barney softly as Dandelion chased her own tail, and then the two dogs, clearly copying her, began to do exactly the same thing. Round and round they spun, the little cat a black and white blur, until they collapsed together in a tangle of tails and paws and ears, and all fell fast asleep.

'If I hadn't seen it with my own two eyes, I'd never have believed it,' said Wilf. 'They're clearly the best of friends.'

KIDNAPPED!

'Boo hoo hoo! Waaugh! IwantitIwantitIwantit!'

On returning to their own house later that day, Cannibal and Bruiser heard a horrible howling noise coming from the cellar. It sounded like a very small child throwing a temper tantrum, but the voice was too loud and too deep, and they knew it meant trouble. They tried to sneak away but just as they were passing the cellar door, it flew open.

There stood Jasper. His face was purple and his eyes were bulging with rage, so that it looked as if they might pop clean out of his head at any moment and roll across the floor. 'S'not fair!' he screeched. 'I wanted that one more than anything else and I didn't get it. IwantitIwantitIwantIwantitIWANTIT!!!' As he stopped to draw breath, he noticed Cannibal and Bruiser. 'It's all your fault, you stupid beasts,' and he picked up a heavy glass paperweight from a nearby table and threw it at them. 'I took you with me and you were worse than useless! You were supposed to help me and you didn't!' He looked around for something else to throw at them, but the two dogs got offside fast, and stayed hidden for the rest of that day.

Now if you own a cat or if you know someone who does, you will probably know that all cats like to hide in boxes. Dandelion, although a most delightful cat, was also quite ordinary and unexceptional in many ways. And so the following morning when she found on the lawn of Barney's house a large empty cardboard box she did what any cat would have done: she hopped straight into it and sat there purring.

All of a sudden – *Flop! Flop!* Someone closed the flaps of the box over her head and the bright yellow sun disappeared. Was it Wilf? Was he teasing her? Dandelion sat quite still, waiting for him to open the box again so that she could tease him, and spring out unexpectedly like a furry jack-in-the-box. But instead of that, she heard the noise of sticky tape as the box was sealed shut and then someone picked it up and carried it off.

What on earth was happening? When the box was opened again, would she be in the surgery, face to face with that nasty vet holding an even bigger bottle of yellow pills and a red leather harness that was stronger and stouter and even more uncomfortable than the one Dandelion was already wearing? But when Wilf was taking her to the vet, he always told her so. 'I'm sorry about this, my little friend,' he would say as he set her gently in her travelling basket, 'but it's for your own good.' Never once had he sneaked up on her and trapped her in a box, carried her off as she was now being carried off.

There was the sound of a car door opening and the box was set down so roughly that Dandelion fell over. It was pitch black and even though she could see in the dark it was no use, because there was absolutely nothing to see in the box. As the car moved off she started to wail and mew in fright.

After a short journey the car stopped. The box was picked up again and carried off. Still Dandelion had no idea where she was or what was happening, except that at last she was taken down a flight of steps. *Riiiippppp!* The tape was torn off and the box turned upside down. Dandelion fell out on her head. 'Nasty little brute! That'll teach you!' screamed a voice. Then there was the sound of a heavy door being slammed shut and a key being turned in a lock.

The person who had captured Dandelion was clearly so unpleasant that she was happy now to be left alone. Picking herself up, she shook the dust from her fur. 'Now let me see where I am,' she thought, 'and what is to be done.'

On looking around, the little cat discovered that she was in a dark, dank, cobwebby cellar. High above her was a tiny window with iron bars, and the cellar itself was cluttered and untidy. One side of it was full of big boxes, dozens of them. What was in them, Dandelion wondered, other stolen cats? She gave a little mew and listened, but there was no reply.

The other side of the cellar was full of things covered with old curtains. Curious, like all cats, she wondered what they were, and pulled one of the curtains back with her paw to have a peep. But she pulled too hard and the heavy fabric slipped and fell, revealing what was hidden.

Dandelion gasped. She rubbed her eyes with

her paws and looked again. 'Am I dreaming?' she thought. 'Did I fall asleep in the box in the garden and will I wake up at any moment?' But she knew in her heart it was all real and yet still she could hardly believe what was sitting there, immense and beautiful, before her very eyes.

It was a painting. Not just any old painting: it was her favourite, the one of the fine fat silver salmon lying on a china plate. Staring at it, Dandelion didn't know whether to laugh or cry. Looking at it comforted her, reminding her of all the nights she had stood before it with her dear Barney, as they made their way peacefully through the house to the kitchen for their supper. How far off those days now seemed, and perhaps they would never come back again, now that Jasper had stolen all the paintings...

Jasper! Of course! So now she understood where she was. All these strange lumpy objects under the curtains were Barney's paintings. It was Jasper who had kidnapped her and thrown her into the cellar of his house. She remembered the voice that had called her a 'nasty little brute' as he tumbled her out of the box. What would he do with her? The poor cat trembled to think, for she knew that there was no deed too dastardly for Jasper, that he was as mean as a man could be. There was one good thing in all of this she realised; only one but it was no small point. For if she was trapped in Jasper's house, then her two best friends couldn't be far away. She hurried over and stood directly under the barred window so high above her head, opened her mouth as wide as she could and.

'MEEEEEOOOOOUUUURGHAWOOOOOOA GHAEEEEEAMAWAROOO!' It was a risk, she knew, but there was nothing else for it.

'WAAAAAAGHAMMMMAAAAAARRROOOO OMEEEEEOOOOWWWWGH!'

'Dandelion! Dandelion!' Her own name popped up in her own mind like a stray thought and as her heart soared, she looked up to see two familiar snouted shadows at the barred windows. 'Help me!' she pleaded with them. 'Jasper kidnapped me and locked me in here, oh please help me!'

'What shall we do?' asked Cannibal urgently.

'I'm so hungry I can hardly tell you. Is there any way you could possibly find some food for me?'

'It won't be easy,' cautioned Bruiser, 'because

Jasper gives us so little to eat, but we'll find something. Don't worry Dandelion, we'll help you and we'll be back as soon as we can.'

The two shadows disappeared from the window and the cat's mind emptied of all thoughts except her own. Once again, curiosity got the better of her. If half the cellar was full of stolen paintings, then what was in the cardboard boxes? She decided to pass the time while waiting for the dogs to return by finding out.

The boxes at the very top of the heap seemed not to be firmly closed and so she set off, climbing nimbly from one carton to the next until she was at the very top of the heap. Gingerly she lifted back the open flaps with her paw, to reveal hundreds and hundreds of strange metal objects, shiny and quite small, pointed at one end and blunt at the other. What on earth were they? The cat had no idea and she turned to the next box, peeped into that too. But this time she recognised immediately the things they contained. Her fur stood all on end in fright and her eyes grew huge and round.

Guns! Dozens and dozens of long dark guns. All at once Dandelion realised that the little shiny things were bullets. Shocked and afraid, she felt very cold now. She had known that Jasper had a gun because he had tried to shoot her only yesterday, but she thought now of the other boxes beneath these two, and the boxes below that and below that again. What if they were all full of such things – guns and bullets and bombs and grenades? Dandelion scampered down the side of the cartons and hurried to the other side of the cellar, as far as possible from the wretched weapons and as close as could be to Barney's beloved pictures.

She was sitting there with her ears down flat when – *Plonk!* A fish fell on her head. It was a very small fish, about the size of the last joint of Barney's little finger, and she wolfed it down in a single gulp. Oh delicious it was, so delicious after her long hunger, so fishy and cool and fine. True, it was tiny, but look on the bright side, she thought as she licked her whiskers: it had fallen on her head and if it had been as big as the salmon in the painting, it would have knocked her out. *Plonk!* And another little fish fell, this time landing directly between her two paws, and again she gobbled it up. *Plunk!* Another! *Plonk! Plunk!*

Plink! It was raining silver fish in the cellar now they were falling like heavy drops of rain in the rays of the evening sun. There were so many of them and Dandelion laughed for pure pleasure as they piled up around her faster than she could eat them.

'Whitebait. Chef's suggestion,' came a stray thought to her mind and she laughed again.

'You darling dogs,' she cried, 'what would I ever do without you!'

WHERE IS DANDELION?

Barney was surprised when Dandelion didn't come home for her lunch, because it was her main meal of the day under the strict new regime. She was always on time and ate up every last scrap in a twinkling. 'Where can she possibly be?' he fretted.

'That cat wants to teach you a lesson,' said Wilf. 'She's been in a sulk ever since I took her to the vet. I bet she's rubbed herself against someone's ankles and charmed them into taking her home with them. Right this minute she's probably sitting on a rug in front of a blazing fire, with children fussing over her and feeding her all kinds of tit-bits. She'll be back here at tea time, you mark my words.'

But Wilf was wrong. The evening came and night began to fall and still there was no sign of the little cat. Barney wandered around the garden in the gathering dusk, calling her name and peering under rose bushes. 'Puss, puss, puss! Where are you my love? Puss puss!' But it was all in vain. The young couple who used to meet every night under the tree, to watch the lights flow in Barney's windows and then go out again, were astonished this evening. The great house was in total darkness save for two little flames that wandered through the blackness of the garden, flickering gently, as Barney and Wilf searched by candlelight for the lost cat.

Eventually Wilf persuaded Barney to go to bed, but he was wakeful and miserable. He missed the familiar warmth and pressure of Dandelion, who always slept on top of the quilt, tucked into the crook of Barney's folded knees. He was so lonely without her. Wilf himself had a clever plan, and he sat up all night at the kitchen table working on it. By the time dawn broke over Woodford, he had made twenty splendid posters, each one with a photograph of Dandelion glued to it.

'LOST!' it said at the top of each poster in big black letters and then under the photograph was written, 'Small cat answering to the name of

DANDELION. Black with white bib and socks and a white splodge over her nose. Last seen wearing a red leather harness. Much loved and much missed. If you see her, please ring Woodford 6082974.' And then at the very bottom, again in big black letters: 'HUGE REWARD!'

As he finished the last of the posters, Wilf rubbed his nose and hoped that they were all right. He hadn't asked Barney about the reward, but he knew that Dandelion was far more important to him than money could ever be. Wilf wasn't at all sure that Dandelion really would answer to her own name. He thought she was just as likely to come running if someone made soft 'puss, puss, puss' noises, but that was true of most cats, so it wouldn't be helpful to put it on the poster, would it? he asked himself. But when at breakfast time he showed Barney what he had done, he was delighted.

'What a good idea! I don't know why I didn't think of it myself.'

Wilf spent the morning going all over town, nailing some of the posters to trees and fastening others to lamp posts with sticky tape and string.

He asked the woman in the chocolate shop if she would put one of them in her window, where everyone could see it. 'I will of course,' she said. 'Poor Mr Barrington, he must be so worried. Here, give him this box of Woodford Creams to cheer him up, and tell him I'm thinking about him.' The baker was also very sympathetic and took a poster. The last shop Wilf called at was the butcher's.

The Woodford butcher was a famously gloomy man. If you met him on a bright sunny day and said, 'What lovely weather we're having!' he was likely to reply, 'Yes, but I shouldn't be surprised if it rains before long.' If you asked him if he was keeping well, he would say something like, 'Yes, but I hear there's a nasty tummy bug going around that I might catch.' When Wilf went in this morning, he was cutting pork chops, with the air of someone who had known the pig in question and had always thought it would come to a bad end. Slowly he wiped the blood from his hands onto his striped apron, and inspected the poster.

'I'll put one in the window if you want,' he said, 'but it won't do any good. I mean, she's a very ordinary-looking animal, isn't she? There must be dozens of black and white cats in Woodford, so how are you going to tell which one is yours? Maybe she's just run away. Treacherous animals, cats. Never liked 'em. Put your trust in them, and this is how they pay you back.' He picked up his cleaver again and brought it down hard on the meat. Another chop fell away neatly. 'If you ask me, you'll never see her again.'

It wasn't at all what Wilf wanted to hear, and as he trudged home he felt every bit as glum as the butcher. But there was worse to come. Barney was waiting for him at the door in a terrible state of agitation.

'She isn't lost, Wilf. She hasn't simply wandered away. It's worse than that, oh much worse! While you were out, someone put this through the letterbox.'

The sheet of paper Barney held up in his trembling hands looked very odd. Someone had cut letters from newspapers and magazines and glued them down to spell out what they wanted to say. There were capital letters in the middle of some words and lots of crazy spellings. Some of

the letters were even stuck on upside down, but
the message was clear enough and terrible for
Barney and Wilf to see:

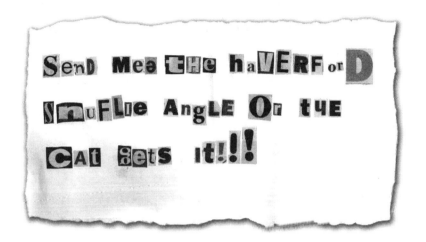

Send Mea the haVERFor D SmuFLue AngLE Or tuE Cat gets it!!!

CANNIBAL AND BRUISER
TO THE RESCUE!

Unlike Barney, Dandelion had had quite a good night. Her belly full of small silver fish, she had fallen asleep curled up in an old curtain before her favourite painting. Thanks to the dogs, she felt as much at home as it's possible to feel when you've been kidnapped and locked up in a dank, cobwebby cellar. In the morning, Cannibal stole a carton of fresh cream from the doorstep immediately after the milkman had been, and pushed it along with his paw to the bars of the cellar window. He nudged it gently through, and it fell to the ground, where Dandelion quickly clawed it open and drank her fill. Bruiser pinched a string of sausages from the kitchen and lowered them down, link by link, to the cat. After she had eaten her breakfast, a thought came into her head. It was Cannibal.

'Now what on earth are we going to do to set you free?'

'Tell Barney,' she replied. 'As soon as he knows that I'm here he'll come and get me.'

'Easier said than done.' This was true. Even Dandelion often found it difficult to get through to Barney, who realised she was trying to tell him something but didn't know what it was. Thinking about it didn't work as it did with the two dogs, and not for the first time she felt sorry that animals couldn't simply talk.

'If we can't tell him, we need to find a way to show him,' considered Bruiser.

'What do you mean?'

'If we could show him, say, a photograph of you with Jasper, then he'd know who had taken you away.'

'That's not very likely, is it?' Cannibal replied. 'She's never had her picture taken with him and even if she had, how would we ever get hold of it?'

'It was just an example.' Bruiser sounded slightly huffy now. 'It doesn't have to be a photograph, it could be a drawing or better still, something belonging to Dandelion. I mean, he knows we're Jasper's dogs, so if we took her red leather harness and showed it to him then he'd be able to work out immediately where she is, wouldn't he?'

There was silence for a moment or two as they thought about this…and then there was total uproar! Both dogs started to bark excitedly.

'That's it! How did I think of it? That's exactly what we have to do!'

'You genius, Bruiser, you clever-clogs!'

Dandelion was thrilled too. 'That's a wonderful idea. There's only one small problem. How do we get the harness off?'

'Can't you just take it off?' Cannibal asked. Dandelion explained sadly that ever since she had been made to wear it, she had spent most of her spare time trying to wriggle out of the wretched thing. She had arched her back in the hope of bursting the leather. She had twisted her head round and tried to chew through the straps. Once she had even climbed a tree and hooked it over a branch, then jumped off, hoping that the weight of her body would make the harness break. But it was very strong, and she had only ended up hanging uncomfortably from the tree for ages, until Wilf saw her and lifted her down. 'I've tried everything,' she said, 'and nothing works.'

'I bet I could chew through it,' Cannibal's thought came to her mind, 'if I could get close enough to you.' He poked his snout further through the iron bars and peered into the cellar. 'Do you see that pile of cardboard boxes? Would you be able to climb to the top of that?'

'Of course,' replied Dandelion, who was nimble and proud of her skills.

'And then when you're at the top, could you stand on tiptoes and stretch as far as possible towards the window?'

'I think so.' She was beginning to feel a little bit more uncertain now. 'And what will you do?'

'I'll get as close as I possibly can as well, and I'll chew through your harness.'

'And I'll be there to make sure that it doesn't fall to the floor, that we don't lose it,' added Bruiser. 'How does that sound?'

'Fine,' replied Dandelion faintly. This was beginning to seem rather frightening to her.

'All right then, let's do it!' cried the dogs.

Imagine for a moment that you're a small black

and white cat who's been kidnapped. Your toes are sore because you're leaning so far forward, trying not to fall off the pile of boxes, all crammed full of bullets and bombs, on which you're perched. An enormous black Alsatian dog has its snout right on your shoulder, and is slowly and carefully chewing through the red leather harness you're wearing. Even if the dog was your friend, even if you squeezed your eyes tightly closed but could still feel it slobber and drool on your fur, and hear the crunch of its sharp, shiny fangs, tell the truth now: wouldn't you be at least a little bit afraid?

Poor Dandelion was absolutely TERRIFIED. All at once, Cannibal stopped chewing. 'Open your eyes,' the thought came to her mind, and she did so. The green eyes of the cat stared straight into the soft brown eyes of the dog. How gentle and kind they looked!

'Trust me, my darling,' Cannibal whispered. 'We love you dearly. I know this must be horrible for you, but there's no other way to get you out of Jasper's clutches.'

'Oh my dear friends, I love you too!' cried Dandelion. 'How good you are to me!'

'I've almost finished, a few more moments should do it. Close your eyes again, my dear Dandelion. Be brave. Bruiser, move in close please to grab the harness as soon as I break through it.'

The dog began to chew again, but the cat now felt happy and calm. 'Almost there, almost there…' Dandelion felt the red leather harness fall away from her and in that very instant two things happened. Bruiser's snout snapped through the iron bars to catch it and Dandelion, losing her balance, tumbled straight down to the floor of the cellar, upsetting all the boxes!

Dazed, she stood up and shook her head, rubbed her eyes with her paws. Far above her was the barred window of the cellar, completely out of reach now, and scattered all over the floor were upended cartons from which spilled hand grenades, bombs and pistols. But what if Bruiser had missed? What if the harness had fallen to the cellar floor too, how would she ever be able to pass it to the dogs to show to Barney? She craned her neck and narrowed her eyes, stared hard. Far above her head, silhouetted clearly against the sky was Bruiser, and hanging from her mouth…the straps of the red leather harness!

'Yes! Yippee! We did it! We did it!' the animals cried to each other in delight. 'Hurrah! Hurrah!'

But now came the next big task – trying to make Barney understand what had happened.

IN THE POLICE
STATION AGAIN

'Whoever's behind all this must be really thick,' Wilf said.

'You mean because they can't spell?'

'No, because they tell you to send them the Haverford-Snuffley Angel, but they don't say where you're supposed to send it.' Wilf was about to pick up the strange letter again when Barney stopped him.

'Maybe there are fingerprints on it,' he said. 'Maybe if we took it to the police they might be able to find out who sent it, and then we'd know where Dandelion is.'

'The police told us to get lost,' Wilf reminded him. 'I don't fancy going there again.'

'Neither do I,' admitted Barney.

Sighing, Wilf glanced up from the letter and

looked out through the window of the room in which they were standing. What he saw there shocked him more than anything he had ever seen before in his whole life. He gulped. He trembled. His face went completely white and his hair shot straight up on his head in wild tufts. 'Woooooohhhh!' he wailed. 'Look, Barney, look! They've eaten Dandelion!'

He pointed a shaky finger towards the garden, where Cannibal and Bruiser were now sitting on the grass, with the red leather harness placed neatly in front of them. 'Every last little scrap of her, down to her tail and her whiskers. They couldn't eat her harness because it was too tough, and so they've brought it here to show us and to gloat. Oh poor little Dandelion cat, we'll never see her again!' And with that Wilf began to bawl and roar.

'There, there, don't cry so.' Barney had never seen Wilf so upset. He took a handkerchief from his pocket and passed it to him. As Wilf snivelled and sobbed and blew his nose loudly, Barney gazed at the two dogs. They weren't snarling or barking. They didn't look vicious and wicked, but gentle and sweet-natured. Cannibal stared deep,

deep into Barney's eyes, put his paw on the harness and gave a little whimper.

'Wilf,' Barney said slowly, 'I think you're completely wrong. These dogs haven't eaten Dandelion. They would never do a thing like that, they're her friends. Don't you remember, they were playing together only the other day.'

'Well where is she then?'

'I don't know,' Barney admitted, 'but there's only one thing for it: we must go back to the police.'

'What! You again?' cried the policeman as the little group marched into the station. 'I thought we told you not to come back.'

'But look what lovely dogs they've brought with them this time,' said the policewoman, 'instead of that horrible cat.' Leaning over the counter, she rubbed Cannibal between the ears and he whacked his tail on the floor with pleasure. 'Good boy! Good boy!' Like Dandelion's vet, the policewoman was someone who preferred dogs to cats.

'It's actually my cat I've come about,' Barney said apologetically. 'Someone's kidnapped her.'

'Maybe the rolling pin that wears lemony-pineconey *eau de cologne* and pinched your paintings took your cat too,' said the policeman, and he chuckled.

'There is a connection,' Barney said, and he took out the letter and showed it to them, together with the red leather harness. For the first time the police appeared to be interested. Suddenly the policewoman said, 'I know those dogs! It's Cannibal and Bruiser, Mr Jellit's Alsatians. There's not a week they don't have their pictures in the *Woodford Trumpet*. You're not suggesting he's at the back of this, are you?'

'I honestly don't understand how it all adds up,' Barney admitted, 'but I do think that's where we should start looking.'

'You do realise that Mr Jellit's a very important man,' the policeman said sternly. 'If it turns out he has nothing to do with all of this, you're in big trouble, you are. I'll charge you both with wasting police time.'

'We should go over there anyway,' said the policewoman, 'and bring his dogs back to him. I'm sure he's worried sick about them, and can't wait to see them again. You may as well come too.'

And so Wilf, Barney, Cannibal and Bruiser hopped into the back seat of the big white car behind the policeman and policewoman, and with lights flashing and sirens wailing, they sped off through the streets of Woodford.

AT JASPER'S HOUSE

An overworked and weary butler opened the door to them at Jasper's house, and showed them into the front room. 'Please take a seat,' he said, swallowing a yawn. 'I shall tell Mr Jellit you're here, and he'll be with you in a minute.'

'Gosh, it's really posh, isn't it?' said the policeman admiringly, looking around at Jasper's blue silk sofas and glittering chandeliers. 'I'm always reading about Mr Jellit's parties in the paper, but I never thought I'd get to see where they actually happen.'

'Oh look,' said the policewoman. On a spindly table was a white china dish decorated with butterflies, and full of sweets. 'Woodford Creams! Imagine being able to have those sitting around in your house every day in the year! We only ever have them when it's my birthday.' There was fudge in the dish too, and sugared fruit jellies. 'Such a pretty dish as well.'

Just then, the white double doors at the end of the room split open and Jasper breezed in, looking every bit as stylish as his house. As he walked past them, there was a strong smell of *eau de cologne,* like lemons and pinecones. Barney and Wilf looked at each other in astonishment and raised their eyebrows, but said nothing. They could see that the policewoman had noticed it too.

'Nice aftershave,' she murmured, and Jasper heard her.

'Thank you, darling,' he said. 'No one else in the whole world has *eau de cologne* like this. It's unique. Like me!' And he gave her a winning smile.

'Hello, Mr Jellit. Let me introduce Mr Barrington and his friend, Mr Wilson. They found Cannibal and Bruiser over at their house,' the policeman said.

'I'm sure you're delighted to have the dogs back, they're such wonde—'

But before the policewoman could finish, Jasper had clipped Bruiser around the ear, and lobbed a kick in the direction of Cannibal, who yelped and ran off to hide behind a sofa. 'Nasty brutes!' he cried. 'I'll give you what-for later tonight. I'll teach you to run away from home, and get into trouble with the police, you see if I don't. Thank you for bringing them back. You can all go now, I'm rather busy, if you don't mind. I'll get the butler to show you out.'

'Not so fast, please,' said the policeman as Jasper moved to ring a small silver bell. 'You see, at the same time you lost your dogs, poor Mr Barrington here lost his cat. Little black and white cat. Nettles, I think you said its name was.'

'Dandelion,' Barney gently corrected him.

'That's right, I remember now. Dandelion. Know anything about where she might be, Mr Jellit?'

'Absolutely nothing. Now if you please—'

'But you see poor Mr Barrington here has been having a really horrible time,' went on the policeman, interrupting Jasper. ''Cos as well as losing his cat, he had lots of beautiful paintings in his house, and someone's gone and pinched those as well.'

'And we, the police, happen to think that whoever has his cat also has his paintings, and so if we could find one, we could find the other,' said the policewoman.

'Do you indeed?' said Jasper. 'Aren't you a clever girl to have such an interesting idea? Anyway, what's a pretty little thing like you doing in the police? You should be a film star! I've an idea, I'll throw a party next week, and invite all sorts of people from Hollywood. Why don't you come along and I'll introduce you—'

'To get back to Mr Barrington's cat,' said the policeman, interrupting Jasper again.

'And his paintings,' added the policewoman.

'Oh snakes' elbows! Who cares?' said Jasper crossly, losing his temper. Then he remembered that Barney was actually there in the room before him. 'Look Mr Barrington, I'm sorry for you, but you should be more careful with your things and you aren't going to find them by standing here. Go home and look again, more carefully this time. I don't know where your miserable cat is, nor your rotten paintings.'

'Mr Jellit,' said the policeman, 'I don't believe you. I think that's a great, big, fat fib.'

'No it isn't.'

'You see, when you join the police,' said the

policeman, 'the first thing they do is to give you this,' and he held up his whistle. 'And the second thing they do is to give you this,' and he held up his baton. 'And the third thing they do is to teach you how to know when someone's telling you lies and you, Mr Jellit, are not telling me the truth!'

While all of this was going on, everyone had forgotten about Cannibal and Bruiser. They didn't notice when Bruiser sidled over to the table where the dish of sweets sat, until the moment when she jumped up and with an almighty crash sent the whole thing flying: table, dish, jellies, fudge and Woodford Creams.

'You wretch!' screeched Jasper, and he lunged towards the dog, but she had already started to gobble up squares of fudge.

And with that, Bruiser simply disappeared.

Everyone in the room gasped, except Jasper, who said something extremely rude, and then the policeman and policewoman looked at each other.

'So that's how he did it!' the policeman said.

The policewoman turned to Cannibal and spoke urgently. 'Where's the cat? Good boy! Good boy! Show us where the cat is.' Cannibal immediately turned and ran out of the room.

'No!' shrieked Jasper, but they all followed the dog, who led them straight to the door of the cellar.

'Locked,' said the policeman, trying the handle. 'Open it at once, Jellit.'

'Why, this is ridiculous,' said Jasper, and he laughed, smiled flirtatiously at the policewoman. 'You don't want to go to my cellar. A little sweetie-pie like you would hate it down there, for it's full of nasty spiders. Why don't we all just go and have a glass of champagne instead?' But he knew it was no use. The policewoman bopped him hard on the head with her baton.

'Listen, Mister, let me set you straight on a few points. I am not your darling. I am not a pretty little thing. I am not your sweetie-pie and above all else I AM NOT AFRAID OF SPIDERS! Now open this door immediately!'

Whimpering, Jasper took a long iron key from his pocket and unlocked the cellar door.

Dandelion thought she was dreaming when all of a sudden, there at the top of the steps was Jasper, the policeman, the policewoman, Cannibal, Wilf and...Barney! With one enormous leap she was in his arms, snuggling and cuddling up, purring and being petted more than ever before in all the time since the first day Barney found her, patting the dandelion clocks with her paws. He slipped her down the front of his cardigan and the little cat knew that she had come home.

The police thought that they were dreaming too, to see the floor of the cellar littered with bombs and bullets and guns, simply hundreds and hundreds of them, scattered from the upended boxes. And in the middle of it all, a beautiful painting of a salmon! The policewoman hurried down the steps and pulled away all the old curtains to reveal every last one of Barney's stolen pictures.

The policeman turned to Jasper. 'Mr Jellit,' he said politely, 'I made a mistake. I told you that when you join the police, the first thing they do is to give you a whistle. It isn't true.'

'No?' said Jasper.

'No,' said the policeman. 'The first thing they do is to give you these.' And taking out a pair of shiny silver handcuffs, he snapped them smartly on to Jasper's wrists.

A REALLY GOOD IDEA

As I told you right at the beginning of this story, all the people who lived in Woodford thought of it as a most unremarkable little town. Imagine, then, their astonishment when they heard of the extraordinary events that had been unfolding in recent days. There was so much news in the *Woodford Trumpet* the morning after Jasper's arrest that it was ten times thicker than usual, and all the paperboys had great difficulty stuffing copies through the letterboxes.

As in every house in town, the butcher and his wife sat reading at the kitchen table over breakfast. The butcher was in his string vest, his wife in a short frilly nightie with curlers in her hair, and both of them were boggle-eyed with amazement.

'A secret bomb factory hidden in the woods! Who'd have thought it? If anything had gone wrong, the whole town could have been blown to pieces,' said the butcher.

'And Barney Barrington having all those wonderful paintings in his house and none of us ever knowing about it,' said his wife.

'Magic fudge!'

'Jasper Jellit an art thief!'

'And a cat-napper! You couldn't make it up.'

'And above all, Jasper isn't even his real name. It's Jimmy!' They read and marvelled as their bacon and eggs grew cold on the plates before them, and their cornflakes turned to a wet mush.

But there was another surprise to come in the newspaper the following day with a huge black headline that covered most of the front page:

'GENEROUS GENIUS GIVES GOBSMACKING GIFT!

'BRILLIANT Barney Barrington has made the EXTRAORDINARY decision to give ALL his paintings to the town of Woodford. In an EXCLUSIVE interview with the *TRUMPET* the marvellous musician told our reporter, "I was UPSET when the pictures were STOLEN and then I lost my cat DANDELION too. I began to think about what was really IMPORTANT in life. I realised that perhaps I'd been SELFISH keeping the pictures all to myself. And so when the POLICE found them for me, I decided that I would GIVE them to the ART GALLERY. I can go down to SEE them every day if I want, and EVERYBODY in the WHOLE TOWN will be able to see them too. I asked Wilf what he thought and he said that it was A REALLY GOOD IDEA."

'Philomena Phelan, Director of the Woodford Art Gallery said, "It's INCREDIBLE. They're MAGNIFICENT pictures. We're going to have one of the BEST collections of paintings in THE WHOLE WORLD. Mr Barrington has been amazingly KIND and BIG-HEARTED in doing this. To THANK him and to CELEBRATE, the gallery and the town are going to throw a HUGE PARTY for him on FRIDAY. EVERYBODY is WELCOME. It's going to be an UNFORGETTABLE night!"

'And the *TRUMPET* will be there too! Don't miss our SPECIAL SATURDAY SUPPLEMENT! BARNEY, YOU'RE A HERO!'

THREE CHEERS FOR
BARNEY BARRINGTON!

But Barney didn't want to go to the party. 'I can't,' he wailed to Wilf early on Friday evening.

'You can't not,' said Wilf sternly. 'Everybody will be so disappointed if you're not there. Go upstairs and put on your best suit.'

Barney hadn't worn his dinner jacket since he stopped giving concerts. When he took it out of the back of the wardrobe, it was full of holes, for the moths had chomped and guzzled their way through the sleeves. Barney had become fatter too, because of all the delicious food Wilf prepared for him, so his tummy pushed the waistband out and made the trousers short in the legs. 'We'd better try to make you look smart,' he said to Dandelion, and put a black velvet bow-tie around her neck. 'There now, it goes nicely with your bib.' But Dandelion didn't agree.

'I look like a waiter,' she thought as she stared at her reflection in the mirror. 'People will keep asking me for drinks and crisps and nibbly things.'

With that there was a knock on the door, and Wilf came in. 'The taxi's here,' he said. 'Blimey, the old suit's seen better days, hasn't it Barney?' Then he noticed the cat. 'You look like a waiter,' he said with a chuckle. 'People will keep asking you for drinks and crisps and nibbly things.'

'Oh no!' thought Dandelion. They heard the toot of a car horn outside.

'No time to waste,' said Wilf. 'Let's be off.'

In the taxi on the way to the art gallery, Barney was so nervous he had a pain in his tummy. He remembered his first day back in Woodford, when he had gone shopping in the supermarket and everyone had stared and pointed at him, as if he were some kind of monster or freak. What if the same thing happened tonight? As he got out of the taxi at the art gallery he noticed that Dandelion was shivering, and as Wilf paid the driver, he picked the cat up in his arms and cuddled her. 'It'll be all right, Puss,' he said, but he wasn't at all sure that it would be. 'It'll be all right.'

The windows of the gallery glowed brightly in the darkness of the night and as they approached they could hear the buzz of voices, the sound of laughter and the clink of glasses. The great wooden doors of the gallery swung open, and…what a sight met Barney's eyes!

There were his paintings – the fine fat salmon on a china dish, the seascape, the young man in the velvet hat, and the rest of them, all wonderfully displayed and perfectly lit. So many people there too, and they turned and stared as Barney, Wilf and Dandelion came into the room. For a moment there was complete silence. And then they started to clap their hands.

The applause grew, louder and louder, and on and on it went, and suddenly Barney felt that he was back in the good old days. It was like the end of a concert, when he knew that he had brought beauty and joy into the lives of hundreds and hundreds of people, had given them something magical that they would never forget. Such moments had always made Barney joyful, and as he no longer gave concerts, he had thought never to know such an evening again. His heart warmed and glowed within him, and as the applause finally died away, someone shouted: 'Three cheers for Barney Barrington!'

'Hip! Hip! Hooray!

Hip! Hip! Hooray!

Hip! Hip! Hooray!'

Goodness, everyone was here tonight, and everyone wanted to talk to Barney. Here was Mrs Haverford-Snuffley in a remarkable hat with a long pink feather in it, from the end of which dangled a bat. The bat was wearing an elegant bonnet, tied firmly under its chin with a green ribbon to stop it from falling off when the bat was hanging upside down.

'So you're the wonderful man who bought my angel,' cried Mrs Haverford-Snuffley. 'Our house is delightful now, isn't it, sweetie?' and the bat nodded in agreement. 'We're all as warm as toast and all the bats have bonnets and berets. You must come and visit us. Do! Do!' And Barney promised that he would.

A young couple holding hands came up to him and said, 'Mr Barrington, we want to thank you. If it hadn't been for you, we would never have met.'

This puzzled him. 'Perhaps there's some mistake,' he said. 'I don't think we know each other.'

The woman laughed, and explained how she had first met her companion under the dripping tree, watching the lights in Barney's house. 'We're getting married next week,' she said. 'Will you come to our wedding?'

'Why of course,' he replied, beaming. 'Congratulations! I wish you many, many years of happiness together.'

Just at that, Dandelion started to paw at his ankles. 'What is it, Pussens?'

Cannibal and Bruiser! There they were, together with the policeman and policewoman. Barney followed as the cat scampered over to them, and the dogs licked her face, snuggling up to her. Although Barney didn't realise it, while he was talking to the police the animals were also chatting excitedly amongst themselves.

'We're detective inspectors now,' the policeman said proudly. 'We both got promoted after the Jellit case.'

'How wonderful! I don't know how to begin to thank you for finding my cat and my paintings. How on earth did you do it?'

'The aftershave made me suspicious,' the policewoman said, 'and then when I saw how mean he was to his dogs I knew he was a bad egg, and so everything followed on from there. Of course, we couldn't have done it without Cannibal and Bruiser.'

'Where have the dogs been living since Jasper was arrested?'

'In the dog-pound. I don't know what's going to happen to them. I'd adopt them myself only I'm out at work all day, and my garden's too small,' said the policewoman.

'Why then, they must come and live with us,' said Barney immediately, and with that the dogs started to bark and bark excitedly. Dandelion began to purr, so loudly that she could be heard even above the noise of the party and the *Plooff! Plooff!* of the *Trumpet's* photographer's flashgun.

'Aren't animals strange,' said the policeman. 'You'd almost think they knew what we were talking about.'

Suddenly a woman appeared at Barney's elbow. 'Hello, Mr Barrington. I'm Philomena Phelan. I hope you're enjoying the party.'

'Oh I am, much more than I thought I might,' Barney said.

'Why, you have nothing to eat or drink,' she said. 'That will never do.' Smiling, she called over a waiter carrying a silver tray. Wilf was also standing nearby, with a great big grin on his face.

The nibbly things on offer were most unusual. There were tiny pieces of toast, each no bigger than a stamp and on each one were…three baked beans! 'I remembered reading in the paper once that you don't like baked beans but Wilf told me that it wasn't true. He told me that you love them,' said Philomena, 'so we had these made especially for you.'

'How thoughtful!' said Barney. 'But these other ones, they're made of fish, aren't they? Raw fish. Are they for the cat?'

'She can have some if she likes,' said Wilf, 'but not all of them, because there's somebody else here tonight who also likes raw fish. Look behind you, Barney.'

Standing behind him was an elderly woman with soft grey hair. She wore an emerald green silk kimono and in her hands she held a white bird made of folded paper.

'O-Haru!'

Barney said her name, but he could say nothing more, because his heart was so full.

O-Haru smiled and bowed, handed him the paper bird.

'We wanted to do something special to thank you for being so generous in giving all your paintings to the town,' said Philomena Phelan. 'So I asked Wilf what you might like, and he said he thought that more than anything else in all the world, you would like to be with O-Haru.'

'He was right,' whispered Barney. 'Oh, my love, I had thought never to see you again. For how long will you stay?'

'For how long do you wish me to stay?' asked O-Haru.

'For the rest of our lives,' said Barney. 'Forever.'

THE END OF THE STORY

And what of Jasper? Together with Mr Smith, he was sent to jail for a long, long time. None of the other prisoners ever knew that Mr Smith had a gold tooth because he never smiled, not even once, in all those years. To begin with, Jasper sulked and huffed. There was no point now in complaining about being given jaffa cakes when you wanted chocolate fingers, because there were no biscuits at all in prison. But he soon settled down, and within a week had made pets out of two rats. He calls them Fleabag and Toe-rag, but unlike Cannibal and Bruiser the rats love their names, and they get along famously with Jasper. He's due to be released from prison any day now and I'm afraid he may well be up to his old tricks again in no time at all...

The dogs were given new names as soon as

they went to live in Barney's house. Cannibal became Prince, and Bruiser became Cuddles. They weren't exactly the names they had wanted for themselves. Together with Dandelion, they still sometimes find it hard to let Barney know precisely what they want to say. But before long, they liked these names even better than the ones they had chosen. Prince was a Prince amongst dogs, and Cuddles...well, the name speaks for itself.

People from all over the country and then from all over the world came to visit Woodford and see its magnificent paintings. They bought Woodford Creams to take home as presents for their friends, so many that the shy, dreamy woman who made them was able to open three more shops. She needed lots more roses to make all the chocolates and so she planted an immense new rose garden, which was so spectacular that in time visitors came to see that too. They also went to see the stained-glass windows in the old church that didn't show angels or saints, but wild flowers: primroses in one pointed window, violets in another, harebells in another, and so on. New hotels and restaurants were built for all the visitors, and so thanks to Barney the whole town became prosperous. Woodford became famous throughout the world as a delightful place to visit, and no one ever again thought of it as dull or unremarkable.

Wilf found a new vet for the animals, someone who loves both cats *and* dogs. Dandelion never again had to wear a stout red leather harness, nor swallow enormous yellow pills.

Every day Barney took the dogs for a walk, with Dandelion carried down the front of his cardigan, her little face peeping out above the buttons. Often he stopped to talk to the local children, who patted the cat's head and stroked the dogs. He went to the art gallery to see all the paintings, and sometimes had a cup of tea with Philomena Phelan while he was there. He did keep one painting for himself – the Haverford-Snuffley Angel – but every January he loaned it to the art gallery so that everyone could see it. This was a good idea because unless you happen to have your birthday in January, it's rather an unexciting month, and so it gave the people of Woodford something to look forward to after Christmas. Together with O-Haru, Wilf, Dandelion, Cann—oops, sorry, Prince and Cuddles, Barney lived happily for many, many years to come and was never lonely again.

One day towards the end of his life when Barney was an extremely old man, the mayor of Woodford came to visit. 'You've done so much for the town,' he said, 'that we should like to put up a statue in your honour.'

'Oh I don't think that's necessary. I'd rather prefer it if you didn't.'

'But we want you to be remembered!' cried the mayor.

Barney gave a little smile. Perhaps he was thinking of Albert Hawkes.

'It doesn't matter whether you're remembered or forgotten,' he said. 'It doesn't matter what people think of you. The important thing is how you live. It was only in giving away all my pictures that my life became truly happy. I found O-Haru again and made many new friends. I found riches I had never dreamed of. No thank you, really, I don't need a statue.'

*

And to this very day if you go to Woodford you will search in vain for a statue of Barney Barrington, but because of his kindness and generosity to the little town he has always been remembered, remembered and loved.

THE END